HALE MAREE

MISTY PROVENCHER

DEDICATION

This one is for Michelle Leighton.

Thank you for all your help and friendship, Michelle.

Our discussion inspired my Hale Maree.

Hope you enjoy mine as much as I enjoyed yours.

CHAPTER ONE

"WE GOT ENOUGH FOR TWO, don't we?"

This is how my father comes in the door that night, yelling and drunk, but laughing. I don't mind him so much when he's like this. I call it beer-drunk. Beer-drunk is when he drops the dishes, but doesn't mind that they're broken, spills things, and grins like his face is made of modeling clay. If I have to pick, I'll take this version over the whiskey-drunk one, when he can get angry at the color of the carpet.

"Yeah, Dad," I call back from the kitchen, "there's enough for me and you."

Then I hear the second set of footsteps following my father into the kitchen, and realize what he meant. He meant company. A man, who would probably be considered handsome, when his eyes weren't so blood shot, comes in behind my father. I never know who my dad might bring home, but it's easier when it's women. None of the men he's brought home have ever succeeded in laying a hand on me, but lots of them have tried, and I've learned to spend the night in my room with a chair wedged up under my door knob. At least, when I get a good look at this guy, he doesn't look like he'd be a creeper. It's not like I ever know for sure, but this guy's smile is friendly, as my dad horseshoes him around the neck with a crooked arm.

"Hale," my dad says, nearly poking out his friend's eye with the indicating jab of his finger, "this here's Otto. From the old neighborhood! We were..."

"At the bar. We were just at the bar." Otto dips his chin like he's correcting a toddler, instead of my full-grown, totally blasted father.

"Yeah, yeah, I know, I know. The bar on Fifth, not Main."

I take a good look at my dad as he staggers toward me. He's got a dark spot around his eye that doesn't disappear when he moves out of the shadows.

"Did you get into a fight?"

Otto shushes my father under his breath. My dad swishes away the admonishment with a flutter of his fingers.

"We got enough, right?" my father asks again, instead of answering my question.

"Yeah, sure," I say, the smile fading. Otto waves his nose over the small saucepan of chunky beef stew that I've got bubbling on the stove.

"Smells absolutely delicious," he says to me. His way of talking sounds kind of fancy, even though he's plastered. Then, to my father, "Your daughter's an incredible cook."

"It's from a can," I say.

"She just turned eighteen. She knows her way around a kitchen," my dad says, and then he breaks into a guffaw, like he's the funniest thing in the world. Otto thinks so too, and the two of them collapse against the fridge, rattling the cookie jar on top. They both look up like it will drop on their heads and start laughing even harder. I scoop the stew into two plastic bowls.

"Watch out," I say, trying to maneuver around them. They manage not to barrel into me, but they're doubled over on each other, still laughing. I dump the bowls on the table and grab a bag of chips off the counter. At least I'll have something to eat when I barricade myself in my room for the

2

night. But, as I walk down the hall, away from the kitchen, Otto says something to my father that turns my face red and freezes me in my tracks.

"So, let's get this settled," Otto says. "She's a good girl, isn't she? You know what I mean."

"Of course she is! What the fuck do you think?" My dad laughs his reply, but there is still enough growl in it that I think I know what kind of 'goodness' they're referring to. What the hell? But then my dad says, "What about Oscar? Good kid? Clean?"

"Hell yes," Otto says. I scoot into the shadows around the corner, as the two men stumble to the dining room table. "He's a man! The girls adore him. He knows what he's doing. That's why I want him to settle down. It's time he starts a family and takes over the business. Especially now."

"Well, if we do this," my father slurps his soup. "Damn it! This shit is hot! Watch it!"

Otto's voice streams from the kitchen, deadly sober all of a sudden. "Jerry, this isn't an 'if' anymore. We left 'if' at the bar a few hours ago."

"I know, I know." My father's hushed voice almost makes it sound as if he's whining. "Loyalty. I got it."

"With our children together, it's like we both have insurance—that you trust me," Otto's voice drops, "and that I can trust you."

The sinister tint in his tone almost erases the words. Their children together? Why are they talking like mobsters? My dad's only got me, so Otto's got to be talking about his own kids, but none of this makes any sense.

"We grew up together, for Christ's sake," my father says. "You know you can trust me, Otto. After everything that happened tonight, you gotta know by now, right? Right?"

There is no answer. I hold my breath in the shadows until my father resumes, feeling only a little better that his voice raises this time, as if he's sliding a bargaining chip across the dining room table.

"But if we do this, Otto, your boy—I don't care what he does with other women, but he better never hit my girl. You hear me, Otto? She comes back to me with scratches even, and I'll cut his balls off!"

"His balls?" Otto laughs. "You're a tough bastard, you know that, Jerry? You don't have to worry. Oscar's not a maniac. He's a soft touch with the girls."

"Not too much of a castlenova," my father laughs, chokes. "I want grandkids, you know!"

"Castlenova?" Otto sputters.

"Yeah, you know! A ladies man, dumbass!"

"Casanova? Is that what you mean?"

The two of them break into peals of laughter, while I stay pressed to the wall, sweating. I have no idea why they're having this conversation, but it totally concerns me, and it sounds like they're planning things they have no right to plan. I just don't get how it fits together, and why they're talking about my goodness, and Oscar's fists, and his Casanova-ness. My father must be even more drunk than he seems. Grandkids! I don't like them talking like any of this is going to happen, and I especially don't like them talking about my baby-making features. It freaks me out in about ten different directions.

"What are you going to do if she doesn't care for him?" Otto says.

"She'll care. I know my kid." My dad's laugh starts to sound like a braying donkey. I'm sick from my stomach up to my jaw, and he keeps hee-hawing. "So, we're business partners now, right?"

"Right," Otto says. They clunk something. I think it's their soup bowls. They've got to be off-the-scales-drunk if either of them thinks that my dad has a business, or is in business, or can run a business. He's been laid off, and collecting state aid, for the last three years.

"We buy the tractor tomorrow," my father says.

"With my money," Otto adds with a slurp.

"And I cut the lawns, with my back."

"Until you build up the business," Otto says. "Then you retire."

"Can't thank you enough," my father slurs.

"We're family, Jerry. Loyal and trusting family, correct?"

"Of course, correct!"

There's a pause, and then, a wet clap of their hands, in what I assume is a handshake on the deal.

"Ok, so let's drink on it," Otto mumbles. "We need to make a toast!"

"There's no toast here," my father says. "There's nothing here but my daughter."

I suck in a breath at the implication, but the two just laugh together.

"You have a beautiful daughter, Jerry!" Otto says. "My son will be very happy to have her as his wife!"

"Of course he will!" my father shouts and laughs as I escape down the hall in absolute panic.

#

Sher picks up my call on the first ring.

"Hey," she says. "What up, my sista?"

"My dad's drunk," I begin, and she yawns.

"So, what's new?" she says. "He didn't bring home another weirdo, did he? You want to come over? I can come get you."

Sher would, too. She wouldn't come over and knock on the door though. Sher and I devised an emergency plan years ago. She comes over, stands under my bedroom window, catches my gym bag, and holds the end of the knotted sheet ladder that I use to escape. We finally figured out, the second time we did it, that we had to weight the end of the sheet with rocks and toss it back through my window, so Mrs. Coley, from downstairs, didn't call the cops about it. One time she did, the cops got my dad for drunk and disorderly, because,

5

when the cops showed up, my dad got even more disorderly about Mrs. Coley calling the cops on him.

"No, listen!" I hiss into the phone. Instead of being mad or hanging up, Sher goes quiet on her end. No one in the whole world knows me like Sher does, and she knows that this is serious if I'm hissing. "He brought home some guy named Otto and, dude...they started talking about my *virginity*. I'm totally skeeved out."

"Holy crap," Sher says. "Ok, I'm coming to get you. You got the chair under your door knob already, right?"

"Yeah, but wait. It's not like *that*. My dad and this guy were talking about going into business together, I think they're...I don't know for sure, but it sounded like they're going to be cutting lawns. They're buying a tractor tomorrow. And then they started talking about me marrying somebody named *Oscar*. I guess it's the guy's son."

"What the fuck?" Sher says. "An arranged marriage? What are they, from the old country now?" She puts on a foreign accent and continues, "I swap you two turkey for my daughter's pussy. Yeah? Yeah? You like? You want?"

I'd answer her, but I was finally getting brain-whomped by what had just happened. Sher keeps going in my absence.

"And what kind of name is Oscar anyway?" she squawks. "That's the ugliest name I've ever heard. Oscar the Grouch, Oscar from the Old Couple..."

"Odd Couple," I correct her distractedly.

"Oscar Meyer Weiner!" I hear Sher slap her own head on the other end of the phone line. "You're not marrying any old Weiner your dad drags home, Hale. I won't let you. You know this kid's got to be a hot mess with a name like..."

"My dad can't do this, can he?" I ask.

"No! Hell no! You're eighteen!" Sher says, but then there's a long pause. "It's gotta be against the constitution or something."

"Even if he's my dad and I'm living in his house?"

"It'd be like sex slavery."

6

"I don't think it's sex slavery if I'm married." My hands are shaking. I rub my damp palms against my knees. "I don't have to agree to getting married though."

"You don't have to do anything you don't want to," Sher says, but her voice is so tiny and scared that a new coat of sweat breaks out on my palms. "You wanna run away and live at my house? I'll come hold the sheet for you."

"Nah," I try to laugh. I can't go live at Sher's. Her family is even more broke than we are. Her mom's trying to raise five kids on her own. When I go there to spend the night, we have to squeeze into bed with Sher's younger sister, who wets the bed when she sleeps too deeply. Sher's mom is nice, but always worn out from work, and too exhausted to sit there and listen to problems that belong to other kids, let alone her own. Even when my dad was thrown in the slammer for his last disorderly, she listened warily for a minute, and then patted my knee mid-sentence and told me I could stay, but, I'd eventually have to bring my own food.

"Maybe they're just talking smack because they're super drunk," Sher says. I can hear the frightened pity in her voice. It makes me cringe. She adds, "Dude, they totally have to be. I mean, who has arranged marriages in the United States? I mean, we are in the new millennium and shit, right?"

#

I un-prop my chair from the doorknob in the morning, but I feel kind of sick. It's that icky feeling of waking up, thinking everything is okay, and then realizing it's probably not. I scope out the hall, listening for foreign snoring or signs of wreckage, but the apartment seems in order and I hear the coffee pot burbling. Someone is around.

I creep down the hall and catch sight of my dad at the table, his head cradled in one hand as he looks over the paper. I let out a relived sigh. If he's looking through the want ads, it's got to mean that all the business talk and backroom-vagina-deals are off. He scours the Help Wanted ads every morning, over his cup of sobering coffee, but gives up by the afternoon and heads off to the bar. It's a familiar rinse-and-repeat cycle.

"Hey, Dad," I say, after I check for visitors and find none. "How are you feeling?"

He looks up from his paper with his sad hound dog eyes, and the father that I love, the one who I stick around for, is here, his coffee mug at his elbow. He never waits for the pot to finish before stealing a cup.

"Hey, honey," he says, motioning to the seat across the table from his, "come talk to me."

"Sure," I say, dropping into the opposite chair. Dad folds the paper and pushes it to the side of the table, takes a deep breath, and lets it out. I hold my own breath, so whatever's left of last night's keg, still on his tongue, doesn't pummel me.

"I got good news," he begins. I lift my eyebrows encouragingly. Sometimes good news means he's found under-the-table work and, sometimes, it means the lights won't be turned off, but the heat will. I wait to hear if there is a bad news chaser, before I commit to any excitement.

"Me and Otto Maree were out talking last night," he says.

"I know. You were here. Eating soup. Remember?"

"Oh yeah." My father smiles and, for a second, his eyes meet mine, before diving back down the length of the table. "Well, we got to talking and we came up with a plan."

"A lawn cutting business, right?" I say, but my gut is doing sick little somersaults. I know they talked about cutting grass, but it didn't seem like that was what they were really talking about.

"Right. Lawn cutting. I guess you heard most of it, eh?"

"Not everything."

"Mmm," he grunts. "Okay, well, I made a decision. Otto's got a good bit of money and..."

"How do you even know him?" My dad always thinks everyone else has a ton of money. I assume it's because, in comparison to us, they do, but even a guy with twenty bucks in a savings account is rich in my dad's eyes.

"We grew up together. Our parents were neighbors, good friends. We were buddies back in the day, but when I left high school to bust my ass in the factories, Maree went off and got his degree. He's done really good for himself. He's got some money, and he's decided he wants to help me out, since we're old friends. He wants to make an investment."

"Dad," I sigh. These investments, no matter who they're with, never work out well. My dad's tried flipping houses that nearly trapped us beneath their epic financial failures. He's sold 'green planet' soaps, magazines, and used computers from the back of his car. He's tele-marketed, and he's collected scrap metal. Nothing's worked, and pretty much every time he's tried, we've ended up a little worse off than we were before.

"I know what you're going to say," he says. "But don't say it. Not this time, honey. This isn't pie-in- the-sky kind of work. This is real, blue-collar stuff. We might not end up rich, but we're definitely going to get ourselves out of the red for good this time."

"Cutting lawns," I repeat, hiking up a doubtful lip. He frowns.

"You got to have some faith in this one, Hale. This is an old friend. Our families go way back, and I know it's going to work. Otto's got money to invest and I've got nothing to do but work, so it's a perfect arrangement. He's gonna set me up with a van, and a trailer, and all the stuff I need to do lawns."

"This doesn't sound right," I say. "What's he getting out of it?"

"Money." My dad shrugs, but he looks away as he sips his coffee. "He just wants to give a good ol' friend a hand, and

I'm taking it, Hale. Damn it, *we're* taking it. And that's another thing I have to talk to you about."

My stomach does a back flip, the kind that fails mid-leap, and my guts fall straight into my feet. I think of the whole Hale's-a-virgin-Oscar's-not-a-beater-let's-have-grandkids discussion from last night. My dad rubs his nose a couple times with his palm. He does that when he's trying to think of how to explain something to me that I'm not going to like. I take a deep breath and start for him.

"I heard you talking to that guy," I say.

"Honey, it ain't what it seems like," he says, rubbing his nose again. "Well, it is, but I made a deal and we're going to do it. Aside from anything else, this is our last chance, Hale. For both of us. It's not like I got a fancy degree. I don't even got my high school diploma. But Otto Maree's got a lot of money and I was in the wrong spot at the right time. This is gonna work out. It can get us both off the state aid, and it can get us on our feet for good. He's got to know he can trust me, so we're forming more than a partnership here, baby, we're forming a family alliance."

That's what they're calling this. A pretty face on an ugly deal.

"Why is it so important that he trusts you?" I ask. My father gets a really distant look in his eyes, like he's looking through my head at the wall. When he doesn't answer, I say, "Are you seriously thinking I'm going to just marry some guy I've never even met?"

My dad straightens up in his chair. His old, blue, terry cloth robe droops to one side. He flexes a fist on the table, and I see the muscles respond all the way up to his neck. My dad's a powerful man, and even though he's never once laid a hand on me, he's put a fist through the wall before. Well, one time. But it's stuck with me and makes me worry that he'll do it again, or that at some point, he'll make a mistake and put it through me.

"You're gonna meet Oscar soon," he says, with a strained, but gentle, tone. He flattens his palm on the table when he catches me staring at his hand. "But this is it, Hale. We're beyond broke. There's nothing. We're going to end up homeless in another couple weeks, unless we figure something out. What's happened with Otto, well, it's awful to say, but it couldn't have happened at a better time for us."

"We can figure something *else* out," I say, but he shakes his head, and I can tell he's not going to give in. He's glued this ridiculous idea to his brain, and there is no pulling it off.

"This is already figured out," he says, his voice dropping to a growl. "It's already happened, and it's not so bad if you just think about it the right way. It's our one chance, and you gotta see it for what it is. You play your cards right, and you won't be eating out of soup cans all your life. You won't have to worry about ever being homeless. You'll have a house and a family and..."

"And a life I didn't want!" I snap. My father rubs his chin.

"Hale," he says softly. My dad, the guy he used to be before my mom couldn't take it anymore and left us both, suddenly reaches over the table and puts his big, bear-paw of a hand on mine. "I'm pretty sure the one we're living right now ain't the one you want either, honey. But this is the best I can do for you."

#

I'm in the truck with a box of lawn-cutting fliers on my lap. My dad got a zillion of them copied off, and he's bent on plastering them all over town. The name of the new company is Simmons and Maree Lawn Services, but due to lack of space, it's now S & M Lawn Services, and I can see loads of problems with that. My father, however, doesn't. He's sitting behind the wheel of a brand new Silverado that we could never afford, even if we stopped eating for a year, and there is a trailer attached to the back, with sparkling new lawn equipment that squeaks as we fly over the bumps in the road. We're going to drop off the lawn crap at Mr. Maree's house and see his loser son, Oscar.

Oscar. The name only conjures up fuzzy green monsters and fat, sloppy, old men now. What kind of name is Oscar anyway? My God, I want nothing to do with this.

My father got me out of bed at eight this morning and announced that we were handing out fliers for his brand new business today. I said, "No." He grabbed hold of my sheets and yanked them off me. He carried them out of my bedroom, and told me I wouldn't get them back until I started cooperating. It's the most we've said to each other since 'the talk' two days ago.

When I finally threw on some clothes and appeared in the kitchen, my father gave me a look up and down, and frowned.

"You aren't going like that," he said.

"Good, because I didn't want to go at all," I said. He sighed. It wasn't one of those 'we'll see' sighs or even a 'you'll see this is for your own good' sighs. It was a 'you better get your ass moving' sigh, and, out of my father, a sigh like that wasn't something to be ignored or argued.

So, I'm sitting beside him, not talking to him, watching out the window, with his massive box of kinky- named, business fliers on my lap.

"This kid, Oscar," my father starts, and I cut him off.

"What a loser name," I grumble. He must be high from the new car smell, because he happily ignores my grumbling and continues.

"Otto says the kid's a looker."

"Of course he did. It's his kid! Who cares anyway? I'm just a cow in this."

"What are you talking about?"

"You're treating me like an animal," I snap. My father looks away.

"I've never met Oscar, but I assume he's a good man."
My father's tone is sober. Maybe he's finally coming to his
senses.

"But you don't really know and you're still telling me to
marry him."

"So you'll have a life!" he explodes.

"That I don't want!" I explode back. I fume out the
window, as my father pulls the truck onto a dirt road that
winds back through trees to a house. No, this isn't just
leading us to a house. We're squeaking down the road of the
Maree's *estate*.

"Nice, huh?" My father lets out a low whistle. "Didn't I
tell you?"

"Tell me that you're trying to sell me down the river in
exchange for a truck and tractor? Yeah, I think you
mentioned it."

He doesn't bother to respond, but instead, steers us to the
epicenter of the half-circle driveway, right at the front door.
He puts it in park.

When my father honks the horn, a chiseled, young man
steps out, onto the porch. While the hard sculpture of his
body definitely catches my eye, it's his dark gaze, sifting me
from this rolling scenery that sends a sharp tingle straight
through the center of my stomach.

The gorgeous stranger moves down the brick steps to my
father's open window and my breath disappears. He moves
like smoke, easy and graceful—like smoke that could get in
my head and make the world seem fuzzy.

He leans his palms on my dad's open window. The
stranger's eyes flick to mine, and his lips twitch a tiny grin of
acknowledgement, before his gaze switches back to my
father.

"You Oscar?" my dad asks. The man nods and puts a hand
through the open window to shake my father's. His eyes flick
back to mine, and pause, as he answers in a dark chocolate
kind of voice, "That's me."

Sludge drops into my stomach, crushing the butterflies. The idea of what my father wants me to do makes any interest I have in the handsome stranger disappear. I turn my face away, looking out the passenger window at the manicured bushes around a ridiculous waterfall. There are three angel statues around the edge. A bright red speck catches my eye. Someone's dressed the middle angel in a pair of striped, red underwear. I snort a tiny laugh.

"I'll just grab my phone," Oscar says. I turn back as Oscar jogs up the front steps and through the front door of his house. Smoke in the wind. I've got to clear my head.

"What's he doing?" I ask.

"Getting his phone."

"I heard that, but why's he getting it?"

"He's coming with us."

"No, he's not." I say, but my father smirks.

"Sure he is," he says. "And from the looks of him, you got nothing to complain about, Hale. He's a nice looking guy. He sounds responsible."

"Because he was getting his phone?" I snap. "Are you serious?"

"Pipe down," my dad growls, as Oscar pulls his front door shut behind him. I move to the middle of the truck bench to make room, sulking and admiring all at once, as I watch Oscar cross in front of the truck. I don't know how he walks like that. Smooth as drifting smoke. I tear my eyes away as Oscar opens the door and gets in next to me.

His weight puffs up the seat and our legs knock together. I glance at him with a ready scowl, but he shoots me a quick grin that says *hi* and *sorry for the leg bump* and I drop the scowl without meaning to. But, then, his eyes scan me and I turn away and level my scowl straight ahead, out the window.

What an asshole.

He's checking me out.

He thinks I'm a cow, after all.

And that's fine with me, because now, he's going to have to deal with one mega-pissed-off bovine.

CHAPTER TWO

WE'RE IN A SUBDIVISION OF nice houses that are not *too* nice, but nice enough to have cash for lawn cutting.

"You two take that side of the street," my dad says, pointing. "I'll go down this side."

"Sure thing," Oscar says. He winks at me. I just grab a stack of fliers and walk away. He follows. I might be the cow, but Oscar's a stupid sheep.

He's on my heels as I reach the first mailbox and stuff a flier between the box and flag.

"Isn't that illegal or something?" he asks. I open the next mailbox, and, while I'm giving him my most sour glare, I whip an entire handful of the fliers into the box and slam it shut. Oscar chuckles.

"Okay, let's do it your way."

"My way," I say, with another fist full of fliers chucked into a box, "is alone. That's my way."

"Oh," he says, with another chuckle. Then, all he does is drop back a step behind me. He's still following me. Like gorgeous smoke. Ugh.

After five houses, Oscar says, "So your dad insisted that you do this?"

He sounds kind of annoyed. I stop, turn, and give him a good look.

"Sucks, huh?" he says, rubbing his arm. He lifts his eyebrows sympathetically. Something about the way he moves his fingers over his skin, or maybe it's how he seems to really agree with me, undoes my anger a little.

"Yeah, it does. I'm glad you think so," I say.

"Hey, if it's got to be done, at least I get to do it with a pretty girl," he says, shooting me another wink. I draw back in horror. *Do it?* Did he actually just say that? He said it so evenly, like it was nothing—is he even serious?

I dump my armful of fliers at his feet and walk away. Moronic sheep. I'm not doing this, no matter what kind of cushy life I'd end up living. I'm not agreeing to anything. I'd rather live in a box.

"Hey," Oscar scoops up the fliers and catches back up to me. I'm charging along, but he doesn't even seem to have to work that hard to keep up. He's just a handsome, dark blob in my peripheral, and I intend to keep him that way. "What did I say?"

"You're actually wondering that?"

"Actually am," he laughs. *Laughs.* Jerk. I keep going, but he keeps up.

"Hey, I apologize," he says. "I've never had a girl go rabid just because I called her pretty, but you're right, I shouldn't have done that. My girlfriend would be furious if she knew I even thought another girl was pretty."

I throw on my brakes so fast that he's a step ahead before he jerks to a stop too. Some of the fliers drop out of his hands and flutter to his feet.

"Oh shit!" He chuckles as he bends to pick them up. And all I'm thinking is that he doesn't even know how right he is.

I bend down and help scoop up the fliers. His cologne is in my nose. He's the deep smell of sandalwood mixed with the fresh smell of apples. I glance up, as our fingers meet on the same flier. Oscar's smile is easy and bright. It's in that second that I realize he's got no idea what is going on.

"So you've got a girlfriend," I say, and Oscar bites his lip with a grin and looks away.

"I do," he admits. "Sophia."

"Pretty name."

"I think so."

"So why are you going around telling other girls they're pretty?" I ask. I don't know why I feel a twinge of jealousy, but I do. It's not like I have to own every cute guy and his compliments, especially this one, but hearing him talk about his girlfriend makes some stupidly competitive part inside me stand up a little straighter. I want to kick myself in the face for it. He shrugs.

"I'm as faithful as they come," he says, spreading his arms with another chuckle, "but I'm not dead."

"At least, not until she finds out," I say.

"True." His wide smile is infectious and I can't help but laugh a little. We turn and walk back toward the mailboxes we haven't hung fliers on yet.

"So what kind of name is Hale? I honestly didn't expect you to be a girl."

"You didn't?" I try not to show my surprise. Maybe Otto really was just too drunk to mean anything he said last night. But it doesn't make sense, why he still bought my dad a truck and a bunch of lawn equipment. Or why my dad is still so bent on pushing Oscar and me together. Unless he just wants to get a rich son-in-law. It doesn't seem right, but it's got to be what's going on.

"Was I supposed to know?" Oscar asks. He's so damn handsome. But, I remember what Otto told my dad about his son being a playboy, so I put another step between us.

"No, of course not," I say, and then, to change the subject, I tell him, "Hale's just a name my father liked."

"Your mom didn't have any say?" He raises an eyebrow.

"Well, I'm sure she did, but she let my dad have his way," I lie. I have no idea if she cared even then, but I know she doesn't care now. She's re-married and lives somewhere in Texas, last I heard. She made a new life for herself, complete with replacement kids and the guy who was once 'the other man' in my parent's marriage.

"It's unique," he says. His gaze lingers too long.

"Thanks, but I bet if Sophia of the Pretty Names heard you say that, she would be upset by it."

"Sophia of the Pretty Names is so busy hanging out with her friends that she might not even notice," he says and I snort. I actually do, and then I think, *who cares*? I can snort all day long. No matter how hot Oscar Maree is, he's got a girlfriend, and no matter how much flirting he does, he's already let me know it's not going any further than this. He's loyal.

So I snort again and say, "She sounds like a catch."

"I've been starting to think that myself," he says, sliding a flier between a box and its flag.

"Don't think it too much. Remember your loyalty."

"I'm only loyal while I'm *in* a relationship." His eyes flash at me, and my stomach does this wobbly thing that could be either wild butterflies, or my instinctual warning system trying to alert me to a predator. Or maybe my gut is signaling both. Oscar pins another flier on a box without taking his eyes off me. "What about you? Boyfriend?"

"Fifty of them," I say. This wins me a full smile. Why do I even want it?

"Huh," he says. "I better be careful then."

"You should. It sounds like Sophia could ignore you to death."

"Yeah, but I was talking about your fifty boyfriends," he says with a grin. I return a sarcastic smile as I pop a flier into a mailbox.

"I heard you're a playboy."

"Did you now?"

"Sounds like it's accurate."

"Who were you asking?" Oscar looks both ways so we can cross the road and work our way up another street. I follow him.

"I didn't ask anyone," I say. "Your father told my dad that."

"That explains everything, then. My father can't stand Sophia. He's been trying to get me away from her since we started dating, three months ago."

"Why doesn't he like her?"

"He doesn't think she's right for me."

"What do you think?"

"I think he's probably right," Oscar laughs, "but I've got to be sure first."

I don't say another word about how our fathers were talking. Maybe it really is nothing. We walk along beside one another, me and the handsome smoke. It's weird how I feel like I've lost something.

"That's tragic," I say. "You should be with the person you want to be with."

"Well," he lowers his voice, as if his father might jump out from behind one of the economy cars parked along the curb. "The truth is, he probably doesn't have to work so hard to convince me. Sophia's a great girl, but I don't think I've been completely sure that she's the right one for me."

A little nerve of panic pops up inside me as he flashes his grin. If he's not with Sophia, and if he doesn't really care what happens between them...oh God.

Our drunken fathers' conversation streams through my head again. I wipe my palms on the back of my shirt, as if I'm stretching my back, instead of getting ready to run away. Not from Oscar exactly—I really don't think he has a clue about what our fathers said—but from his reaction to all the crazy marriage talk, when they tell him. If they tell him. If this isn't just my big misunderstanding of an eavesdropped conversation about goodness and grandkids. Then I think of my dad at our kitchen table this morning, so solemn in his drooping blue terry cloth robe, and I just don't know what to think.

I blink out of my thoughts, coming back to the subdivision street. Oscar is staring at me. His eyes are warm and dark and intense. His gaze delivers a full shot of delicious adrenaline all at once, erasing everything else in the universe, but his eyes. When I finally catch that his lips are moving, I have to concentrate extra hard to remember that there is more to him than the soul that seems to want to explode from his gaze.

"Would you?" His voice is soft, his brow questioning. His hand reaches for mine, but I'm still holding a bunch of fliers. Would I? Alarms go off. Would I what? Does he know after all? Is he planning on getting down on one knee? Why is he still looking at me at like that, and putting his hand on mine, and talking like his voice is made of milk chocolate? Why is he having this effect on me?

"Would I what?" My legs fill up with adrenaline and my muscles are ready to go.

"Would you like to take that side of the street and I'll take this one," he says. Oh, pop. The adrenaline is gone and I look down the row of houses, as if it's actually interesting.

"Yeah, that's fine," I say. "We can get it done faster that way, so you can get back to...whatever."

Oscar pinches his face, like I just swung a bat at his head.

"I don't have anything going on today," he says. "I'm good with spending it out here, walking around. I just figured you had better things to do on a Saturday. Like getting back to your fifty boyfriends."

"Well, yeah, I do need to get back to them," I say, "but we still have to hand out a ton of fliers. No reason to be totally bored while I do it."

"We'll stick together, then," Oscar says and suddenly, I feel as unstable as if I'm standing on the top of a thin fence, flailing to keep my balance.

#

"Where have you been all day? I've been worried sick!" Sher shouts into the phone. My dad finally dropped me off at our apartment and is driving Oscar home.

"I had to hand out fliers," I grumble. "for the lawn business."

"It's for real?"

"I don't know. But I met Oscar and he doesn't seem to know what's..."

"Oh my God! What does he look like?" she gasps. I even hear the wince in her tone, waiting for the bad news. His name is Oscar, after all.

"He's actually super hot."

"Are you serious? A hot Ocker?"

"Did you just call him Ocker?"

"It slipped. I was gonna hope you didn't notice."

I laugh. "I think that's what we should call him from now on. Not to his face though, of course."

"Of course," she agrees. "So you're seeing him again? Are you engaged or what?"

"No, he's got a girlfriend," I say, and that sad little tug I felt before, pulls at the bottom of my stomach again. "I think Mr. Maree was just kidding last night. But I am kind of worried, because I think my dad's still taking it all serious. Something did happen, because Otto did end up getting my dad a truck and a bunch of stuff to start a lawn business. Something's going on, but I don't think it's what I thought."

"What did Ocker say about it?"

"Nothing. I don't think he knew anything at all."

"Maybe it is nothing then."

"That's what I'm thinking," I say. The call waiting clicks. "Sher, someone's calling. I'll call you right back, okay?"

"Yup," she says and I click over.

"Hale?" Oscar's voice sends a quiver down both my legs and back up, meeting in places that shouldn't tingle just because a guy, who has a girlfriend, says my name.

"Hi," I say. I'm about to ask if he left something in the truck as he cuts me off.

"I was wondering," he says. "If you'd meet me at a coffee shop tonight?"

My brain trips over my pounding heart. Did my dad tell him on the ride back to his house? Oscar's voice is so weirdly calm, I'm not sure that he knows anything yet, so I play along.

"Sure, I'll meet you. Are you bringing Sophia?" I ask. He puffs an I've-been-called-out breath on the other end.

"I was thinking I'd leave her home tonight."

"Probably not a good idea, Oscar," I try to joke. "You *are* loyal, remember?"

"I am," he sighs, "but if you are going to be my wife, I guess that trumps any loyalty I have to a girlfriend, now doesn't it?"

I don't know if he says anything else, because I drop my phone and the screen shatters when it hits the floor.

#

I generally cling to the notion that people aren't evil bastards. It's hard to stay on task sometimes and keeping thinking it, like when the girl at my school begged me, in the ladies room, for a buck, so she could buy a tampon from the machine. It was hard, because she didn't use the money for what she said she would, but ended up two people ahead of me in the lunch line ten minutes later, buying a tray loaded with a burger, fries, Coke and two desserts.

It was hard to keep believing when the guy upstairs told the cops my dad was a dealer, to throw them off his own scent. I mean, I try my best to assume that lunch girl really needed the dollar more than I did, and that the guy upstairs just made a super crappy mistake. I believe in karma and, sure, sometimes I even try to kick it in the pants, to wake it up and help it get an eyeful of what's happening, but even when it doesn't come through, I still cling to the hope that people are good, down deep. The prospect of life being full of a bunch of evil people, who are waiting to screw you over the minute you turn your back, is way too depressing.

But today, I am completely pulled under by the idea that the biggest evil bastard of them all is the person who helped create me. There's something really jarring about figuring out that your father isn't just imperfect, but actually evil.

My father walks in ten minutes later and I'm standing five feet from the front door with my arms crossed over my chest. He glances at me and tosses his keys on the dining room table.

"You talk to Oscar already?" he asks.

"You must've given him my number. He called me."

"I figured he would."

"I am **not** marrying a stranger," I tell him. "Whatever you did to make this happen, you have to un-do it. Give the truck back to Mr. Maree and whatever he gave you. If you don't, I swear that I will leave tonight and you'll never see me again, Dad. Never. I mean it. I'll live on the streets if I have to. So, you tell me what you want to do. Should I stay or go?"

My dad rubs his face, exhausted. He motions to the couch, for me to take a seat. He drops into the chair, but I sit at the edge of the furthest couch cushion.

"I'm trying to give you a better..." he begins, but I stop him with a glare.

"I don't want a better life."

"Okay." He rubs his hand over his face again. "Okay. Here's the deal, Hale. I am trying to get you out of this mess. *All* the messes I've made. You got to trust me on this. I can't tell you everything because...because I just can't."

"That's not good enough, Dad. I'm your daughter, and if you can't trust me, then there's nobody else. If you're going to ask me to do something as crazy as this, then I think I should know what kind of trouble you're in."

My dad rocks the chair he's in by pushing his toe against the floor. He moves his tongue around his mouth, staring at me in deep thought while he does it.

"It's not my trouble, but it could turn into that," he finally says. "I helped out a friend and he owes me for it, but having you marry his son is necessary. It's not just giving you a better life with money, but it's also keeping you safe.

"Safe," I repeat. My voice slopes down to a whisper. "Dad, did you murder someone?"

"I didn't do anything, Hale," my father says. "But Otto made a mistake, and I happened to be there to see it. I'm a witness. You understand what I'm saying?"

I realize I'm holding my breath, but I manage to answer, "I think so."

"I saw something I shouldn't have. Otto's not a criminal, he's not, but this *mistake* happened and now Otto could lose everything if anyone were to find out. Otto didn't make this lawn-business deal to shut me up; it's not like that. He's just asking for my help, and he's going to help me out in return."

"He killed someone?"

"I'm not talking about what happened." My father sits back in the chair. "It's better if you don't know anything about it, so don't ask anything else."

"He'll assume you told me. Or the cops will."

"Not if you don't know anything. Nobody can assume nothing. That's why Otto decided that if you're married into his family, it's just extra security for both of us."

"He doesn't think I'd turn in a father-in-law?"

"Would you? Even if it destroyed every shot you've got at having a decent life? Even if it led back to your old man?" My dad's eyebrows hike up.

He caught me. Of course, I wouldn't. I've watched enough mobster movies to understand what's happening. Otto's keeping friends close and his accomplices even closer. But, as far as I know, Mr. Maree isn't a mobster. He's a corporate big wig with a bunch of degrees.

"I don't want this. And Oscar's got a girlfriend, did you know that?" I say. "It'll never work with us. You and Mr. Maree need to figure out something else, and keep me and Oscar out of this."

"It's too late," my dad says. "We already made our deal. If you two are married, Otto would know for sure that I'd never tell. I wouldn't say anything either way, but with you in his family, Otto knows I would never change my mind about going to the cops. And I'd know you'd be safe."

My father shuts his mouth, and I don't open mine. I listen to Mrs. Coley's TV blaring downstairs. If I don't marry Oscar, it means that my father can't be trusted. I've seen enough movies to know what happens to someone who can't be trusted. I hear the air conditioning kick on, and before the air even gets a chance to rush into the room, goose bumps climb up my arms.

"Oscar wants to talk to me," I hear myself say. It's like someone else is talking and I'm miles away. I'm handing over my life in this moment, and I don't even feel like I'm actually there, doing it. What I say next is, "He wants me to meet him for coffee, and I don't know where, because I broke my phone."

My dad frowns, leans to one side in the chair, and pulls his phone off his belt. He holds it out to me, and I take it, meeting his sad gaze.

"Look at this the right way, Hale," he says. "You can look at it good or you can look at it bad, but since it's got to be done, it's best to look and see that you can do it."

CHAPTER THREE

I'M NOT A GIRL WHO doesn't know she's pretty, but I'm also not a girl that broadcasts it. I walk to the coffee shop up the street and sit by the window to wait for Oscar. I stare at my reflection in the glass. I know what I see, but I wonder what Oscar sees when he looks at me. I wonder if it matters. He's got to realize how crazy this is, but his voice was so weirdly calm on the phone, almost blank. That flips me out.

When Oscar pulls up, I am not sure it is him right away. A million people have come and gone with cups of coffee for carryout, so when Oscar finally pulls up and gets out of a silver truck, I'm surprised that I can place his silhouette right away. His shoulders are back, as he walks toward the front door of the coffee shop, like he's just making a coffee run, and not like he's coming to talk about our impending doom. When he steps out of the shadows and through the door, his eyes are already on me. Startled, I look away.

I'm all frightened and shaky inside, so I take my hands off the table and wipe my palms on the napkin in my lap. Oscar gives me a suave wink and a smile when he walks in, but he buys himself a cup of coffee at the counter before walking over and sliding into the seat across from mine.

"Hi there," he says.

"Hi," I say, but what I really want to say is; *you're hot as anything, but I still don't want to marry you. This is your dad's fault. You've got a girlfriend, and I'd like to have a life.*

He leans back in the chair and removes the lid on his coffee. He lays it on the table and moves it around absently with one finger while he stares at it. It makes me uneasy.

"Did you know what was going on when we were handing out the fliers?" he asks. He glances up to see me nod slowly.

"I thought my dad had just been really drunk and got it all wrong."

"Do you know why this all happened?" he asks.

"No," I say, remembering how my dad was so reluctant to tell me. I think it's smart to play stupid, in case Oscar goes back and reports to his father. "Do you?"

"No," he says, and I don't believe him at all. I think he knows as much, or more, than I do, but he's not willing to say anything either. My dark guesses sink inside me. I think Oscar's dad killed someone and that my dad saw it.

I lean over my side of the table and whisper to him, "I still don't think that what they're asking us to do is right and I'm not going to do it. So, you don't have to worry. You just have to let your dad know that my dad can keep a secret."

Oscar takes a drink of his coffee, keeping his gaze square on me. The shiver down my spine isn't attraction. It's pure anxiety, from what I see in his eyes. Resolve.

"It's not that easy," he says, as he puts the cup down. He hasn't moved his eyes a millimeter. He leans in and, suddenly, our faces are only inches apart. The sandalwood and apple scent of him wafts up my nose and calms me. If any one glanced over at us, I'm sure they'd think it was just a couple whispering *I love yous* across the table to each other. But if they were sitting where I am, I'm sure anyone of them would shrivel in their chair at how darkly serious Oscar's eyes appear.

"You have a girlfriend." I whisper the nervous reminder. His eyes flick to my lips.

"I need a wife," he says.

"Then you should marry Sophia," I say. He stands and reaches for my hand.

"Impossible," he says. I pull my hand away, staring up at him, tall and dark, with eyes that would melt me if they were looking at me with desire, instead of resolve. "Come with me."

"Where?"

"We need to talk where it's more private."

The third shiver of the night slips down my spine. "I don't even know you, Oscar. I'm not going anywhere."

"I'm not going to hurt you, Hale," he says, but he drops his hand, and the steel in his eyes blows away like dust. What's left is something sad that makes me listen to him. "Don't be afraid of me. I wasn't expecting any of this either."

And that's why murder victims go willingly, I think. The sad eyes, the soft voice, the boy who seems to have just as much to lose. I stand up, even though I still don't take the hand he offers me, and we go out the door to his truck.

#

"Where do you want to go?" I ask when he starts the engine. His knuckles are tight on the wheel.

"I don't know," he says. "Maybe we can just drive. You still scared?"

"Should I be?"

"No," he says. He pulls into traffic. I look at the dash, the door, the window. I just don't look at him. I don't know what to say to this stranger. We can't really talk about what's happened without one of us revealing what we really know, or really think about what's going on. All I know for positive is that it's not going to be me.

We drive through the side streets, past my street, and he keeps going. He doesn't look at me. He doesn't turn on the radio. It gets really nerve wracking. It turns out, I'm the one who can't take it anymore. I break the silence after all.

"This is messed up," I say.

"Which part?" He finally glances over at me. I shrug.

"Every part," I say, and his lips turn up in an understanding grin. He steers the truck off the road and onto a twisting drive. I know the one. It leads to a park with a track running around the brim of it, a playground on one side, and just grass in the middle so kids can play football or soccer. In the dark, the trees lining the drive look like crowds of warlock giants, waving wands and casting spells as we drive past them. He drives us up to the parking lot near the playground and puts the truck in park. He turns in his seat to face me, resting his back on the door.

"Tell me about yourself," he says. I stare at him blankly. Is this his idea of a date? An interview? I look out the front window.

"I'm really sorry all this happened, Oscar, but I think this stuff about getting married is absolutely nuts. Don't you?"

"No," he says. I swallow. The truck suddenly seems too small and the drive here too far. My hands pour sweat.

"I think you should take me home."

"No, I can't," he says. "I need to get to know you, Hale. This situation is out of control, but it's definitely happening, and I want to know who you are before it does."

I put my hand on the door latch and quickly flip the door open, in case he tries to lock me in. I jump out and run. I hear his door open too. My ears pound as I sprint across the track and onto the grass. I glance behind me. Oscar's right on my heels. He grabs me and I trip. We tumble down onto the grass together.

The adrenaline forces me back up, but Oscar grabs my ankle.

I fall and he jumps on top of me this time, a leg on either side of my ribs, and one hand holding both of mine, his other hand clamped over my mouth. He lowers hischest onto mine and I feel all his muscles tensed against me, trying to hold me down and keep my mouth shut, all at once. I try to land a kick, bite him, and push. Nothing works. Oscar is fast and strong and athletic, and I've spent way too much time being a solitary bookworm.

"Hale!" he says in my ear. "Listen to me! I'm not trying to hurt you or freak you out, but somebody's going to hear!"

"Good!" My reply is muffled through his hand.

"Not good," he whispers back. "If I land in jail, what do you think would happen to your father?"

I go limp. This is how morons get subdued. That, and because I've got an out-of-shape body that is sucking wind through Oscar's fingers, and blowing out snot and air on the edge of his hand. He leans his head down to whisper in my ear again. I feel his chest, his arms, and his guy parts, all pressed against me.

"Listen, I know what happened," he says. "I know why we have to get married and if you want me to tell you, I will, but it's got to stay between us. I'll let go of your mouth, but you have to talk to me...not scream your face off."

"Okay," I muffle into his hand, and he slides it slowly off my mouth. His nose and mine are still too close. "Get off me."

Oscar rolls off and sits beside me on the grass. I sit up and fix my shirt.

"So tell me," I say.

"My girlfriend? Sophia?" he says. "She was cheating on me. She was getting with someone from her work. Rick Tatum. Stupid name, huh?" He shakes his head miserably. He doesn't need an answer. "He came looking for me and found my dad instead, while my dad was having a drink with your father. He didn't realize my dad wasn't me, so he must've been looking for my truck. My dad was using it because his was in the shop. Anyway, Tatum was waiting out back, by my truck. But our fathers left the bar and went down the block to get cigarettes, instead of going right home. They stopped off at another bar, and then, when they came back to my truck, Tatum confronted them in the parking lot.

"Tatum said he was with Sophia now, and that I needed to get out of the picture. Your dad stepped in and Tatum threw down on him. Started really beating on him. My father backed up my truck, trying to knock the guy away from your dad. But it knocked Tatum on his head, and he hit whatever it is that you shouldn't hit.

"But our dads didn't know Tatum died. They were in a hurry to get away from him and thought he was just knocked out. That was bad enough. Considering my dad's business and professional reputation, even knocking the guy out would've probably triggered a huge media scandal. It was reported on the morning news that Tatum was dead. The reporters are saying the guy died, and the cops are calling it a hit-and-run. They don't have any suspects yet, because the bar's security cameras have been busted for a long time, and there were no identifying tire marks or anything. There's not even a scratch on my truck either. Tatum wasn't even found until the bartenders went home, so no one knows exactly when it happened. No one knows and no one ever can. Nobody, but our fathers and us, Hale."

Oscar, in the moonlit park, looks almost iridescently pale. I'm sure I look the same. I remember my dad walking in last night, the black eye, the way Otto shushed him. They thought the guy was just knocked out. My dad got a lawn service and a married daughter, not to tell. But now the guy's dead. I can see how things are not only not going to change, but they just got a whole lot more serious.

"So this guy, this Rick, he was after you?" I say. Oscar nods. "Sophia was cheating on you?"

"It's not such a nice name after all," Oscar says.

"Why didn't she just break up with you?"

"No idea," Oscar shrugs.

"This can still come back on you," I say. "If the guy told anyone where he was going, or Sophia...she would have to know."

"I don't think she does," Oscar says. "She called me before I spoke to you tonight. She wanted to know if we were still going to my dad's beach house. We were going to take a long weekend for Landon's birthday bash."

"Eww," I say with a wince.

"But even if the guy told anyone he was going to the bar to get me, I wasn't there. And Modo, the owner, is one of my dad's friends. He wouldn't say anything, even if he knew something."

"What does your dad do exactly?"

"Investments. Financial planning. He's a Merlin in his field," Oscar says. "You've never heard of Otto Maree Investments?"

I shake my head. "I don't have any money."

"My dad's been responsible for the financial development of several Fortune 500 companies. The media would kick into a frenzy just over the fact that my dad was out drunk and there was any kind of altercation at the bar, but it would be an absolute scandal if they knew he was responsible for Tatum. It would total him out. Clients would run for the hills and the business would hemorrhage. But a death? It doesn't matter that it was accidental, and it wouldn't matter if it was provoked. The possibility of a conviction would likely bankrupt my family...and yours. If my dad goes under, it means yours probably would too."

"Holy shit," I say. Oscar turns his eyes back to mine.

"Hale," he says. "I don't know you, but now you know everything I do. I trust you with it and I want you to trust me too. I want to know you do. Our fathers talked to me about what needs to happen and I think it's the right thing to do under the circumstances. I think that if we are married, both sides have a lot to lose, so we'll all make sure to keep it together. So, I'm asking you, Hale. Will you show us that we can trust you? Will you marry me?"

My brain is gaping as I stare at him.

"Hell no," I say, as I jump to my feet.

#

I run like I'm being chased by a rapist with a full can of mace. I don't think my lungs have ever tolerated that much running, but tonight, they seem to get that they shouldn't let me down.

Oscar shouts my name behind me, but, this time, he doesn't follow me. I brace to be tackled for the first hundred feet and, when I'm not, I unfold and go at a full sprint, darting into the trees.

I get that giving in might sound like a great Godfather kind of deal to them, but the one part of the equation they forgot is that I have everything to lose. I'm a financial aid case right now, but I've always assumed I could land a scholarship, get a student loan, and become a success story at some point. I've never thought of my life as a slow decent down an even darker toilet drain. All my plans have always been aimed at hitting the glass ceiling with a titanium helmet. I want to graduate, to live in a dorm, to date ten guys at once, and break up and make up and, someday, marry a guy who I know loves me. I want to marry someone I know.

When I finally hit the lights of a gas station, I stop a pony-tailed guy who is exiting the store, checking something on his phone as he sucks down a gallon-sized slushy.

"'Scuse me," I pant. The hippy guy looks up like I'm about to ruin his day. "I'm really sorry to bother you, but can I use your phone? It's important."

One edge of the hippy's lip twitches up, as he says, "No."

"C'mon," I huff. "This is serious. I'm trying to get away from..."

"Forget it. I'm not giving you my phone." Hippy says, as Oscar's truck pulls into the gas station.

"Dude! I need help!" I shriek, grabbing for the hippy's phone. He twists away and I end up with my fingertips on his drink cup instead. I yank it from him, but the lid pops, dousing me in cherry slushy just as Oscar rolls up beside us. Oscar leans over and pops open the passenger side door.

"What the hell!" The hippy shouts at me. "What the fuck is your problem?"

Oscar's out of the truck. He rounds the grill and wedges himself between the hippy and I.

"Sorry about the slushy, man," Oscar says. He fishes out his wallet and hands the guy a five-dollar bill. "No harm, no foul, okay?"

The hippy still frowns as he snatches the bill out of Oscar's hand and stalks away. Oscar turns back to me, putting his hand on his open truck door.

"Get in," he says. "I'll take you home."

I shake my head and Oscar groans.

"If you don't, I'm going to follow you in my truck the whole way there," he says. He wobbles the door. "C'mon."

Cherry slushy is dripping into my shoes. He reaches into the back seat and pulls a towel out of a gym bag.

"It's clean," he says. I take it, wipe off, and slide into the passenger seat, defeated. He closes the door and in seconds, he's behind the wheel. He swings an arm over my seat as he backs up the truck. It feels like he's putting his arm around me and I glance over, tracing his arm back to his face. Without moving it, he shoots me a small grin and says, "By the way, I forgive you."

I scowl. "For what?"

"For that moment when you thought I was just like everyone else."

#

He puts the heat on, so the slushy will dry, but rolls down the windows too, because it's June and, technically, too warm to be running the heater. The breeze that comes in is cool, but the warm air from the vents blows right up the legs of my shorts. I finally reach over and turn off the heat.

"Is it making you sticky?" he asks. I squint at his profile, thinking of about fifty ways to tell him what a douchebag he is, when he looks back with such a sincere question peaking his brow that I realize *I'm* being the douchebag.

"Cherry slushy will do that," I say. My cheeks burn as if I've just laid my face on a stove burner. He turns on the music, so we don't have to talk, and I'm taken off guard at how I'm a little bit touched by how gracious he is. I steal another look at his profile. It's frustrating too, that his looks leave little to complain about. He's textbook tall-dark-and-handsome, right out of a department store box. I can tell from the way his muscles flex, as he steps on the brake and moves the wheel, that this is a boy who does his push ups. I'm sure any girl would be happy to be sticky in his truck. At least, that's how I try to explain away the sparks shooting down so low in my belly. I think a blind chick couldn't help being a little turned on by how Oscar looks. It doesn't overrule the fact that I'm still freaked out by the whole marriage proposal thing, but I can't help how a glance at his face numbs it a tiny bit. Or, how the numb hits the exact place that makes me forget why I'm here, and what Oscar really wants from me.

"How old are you, Hale?" His voice startles me as he turns down the radio.

"Eighteen."

"Do you have a boyfriend right now?"

"No."

"Hard to believe," he murmurs. "How long has it been?"

The way he asks, the douchebag thoughts come streaming back to me. "Since what?" His question mark brows shoot up again. "Since you've had a boyfriend."

"Oh, a while," I say. I don't want to tell him that it's been *never.* My dad's not just an alcoholic, but a racist too, and I pretty much go to school with 99% not-my-race boys. I've been kissed a couple times, but there was never anyone that I wanted to go out with so badly that I'd risk my father's wrath. Sher's my only friend at school, and she's not that successful in the guy department either. Being two skinny, little white girls in a school full of curvy, chocolate goddesses who guard their men closely, we've learned to keep our heads down and stay off the radar. It hasn't left me with good odds.

"A while," he repeats, as he pulls into the parking lot of my apartment building.

"How old are you?" I ask.

"Twenty three," he says, finding a spot and turning off the engine. Two and three. I could tell he was older than me, because he wasn't nervous or goofy, but I would never have guessed he was five digits older. Then, like it will change anything, he says, "Well, I'll be twenty-four next month."

It doesn't matter. I wouldn't have guessed six numbers older, either.

"I'll walk you in," he says.

"You don't need to," I say, but as I get out of the truck, so does he. He does a lingering look up and down the lot, surveying the cars on blocks, the duct-taped windows, and the clunkers that haven't moved off their flat tires in months. Our parking lot looks like a scrap yard, but I never noticed it as much as I do now, standing with tall-dark-and-immaculate Oscar and his scratch-free silver truck.

"But I am," he says.

"You're in more danger here than I am," I tell him.

"You really think that, don't you?" The chuckle he adds to it irritates me. We climb the stairs to my apartment door.

"Good night," I say.

"Aren't you going to open the door?"

"I will, when you're gone," I say. Oscar's eyes fix on mine, and I try to hold his intense gaze, but can't. I glance away, taking a step back as he takes one forward, pining me between him and the door.

"Open it now," he says softly. "While I'm here, so I know you got in safe."

When I don't move, he adds, "You don't have anything in there that I haven't seen before, Hale. Open the door."

I turn away, his breath in my hair and his cologne in my nose, as I slide the key from my pocket into the lock. It should be a relief to step inside, but the minute the door opens, I see two of my gym bags and a paper bag full of my belongings, heaped on the floor. My dad looks up from his seat at the table, a half-empty bottle of Jack near his elbow. This is my Whiskey Drunk dad, even though he shoots Oscar and I a wry smile as we come in.

"There's your stuff," he says, motioning to my bags with a sloshing glass. "Go on and go."

"Where do you want me to go?" I ask.

"Somewhere else. Anyplace. Just let it all blow down here. You know. Right, Oscar? Let it all blow down."

Oscar walks over and picks up my two bags, throwing one over his shoulder. I know I shouldn't rock the boat with my dad being full of whiskey, but I don't know what he's expecting me to do. I'm not going to just go live with Oscar. I'm not leaving even the little I have behind.

"Dad, I'm not leaving..."

"To hell you're not!" he slams his drink down, and the amber liquid jumps up like lighter fluid in a fire. "Get out of here! I don't know what's going to happen! But if somethin' does, what'll happen to you, Hale? You wanna know? I'll tell you. You'll be livin' on the street and I'll be servin' life in jail."

"I'll go live with Sher until you're out!"

"You'll go with this *kid*," my father roars. "That's what you'll do. You'll go and do what he says, and you'll have a good life, dammit! LISTEN TO ME!"

My father picks up the whiskey bottle by the neck and throws it. It slams against the wall beside me and shatters, the whiskey splashing on me, some of the splintered glass sticking in my skin. I stare at my father as he collapses at the table, dropping his head into his folded arms. Sobs come out of him like emergency sirens.

Rick Whoever is dead and this is the only protection my father can give me—a near miss with a whiskey bottle—to scare me away.

"Come on," Oscar says, hefting up the paper bag and handing it to me. I take it and follow him out the door, empty. My father's wails follow me down the stairs and trail behind me as I walk toward everything that scares me most.

CHAPTER FOUR

I DON'T ASK AND OSCAR DOESN'T say.

We drive through town to the enormous mansion where I first saw him. He leaves me in the truck, but takes the keys and disappears through the front door. I listen to the tires settle into the gravel as I rub dabs of my own spit on the tiny wounds that came from the shattered bottle. Luckily, there is no glass in my skin, no cuts that need attention. I have enough to worry about already, as I stare at Oscar's empty seat and wonder what the hell I'm going to do next.

He returns quickly, flipping down the tailgate and shoving in another two bags. When he slides into the driver's seat, he does look a little surprised that I'm still sitting there, but it's not like I have anywhere to go. My insides feel caved in, but I won't let one tear slip out of me. I don't have a phone, I don't have any money, and I'm screwed. The deal is done. My father sold me out with a busted whiskey bottle. I get that I'm at Oscar's mercy now, and I figure it's just better to be quiet, and wait for a moment that I can take advantage of.

"How are you doing?" he asks.

"Seriously?" I say with a frown. "I'm doing 'trapped' like a champ."

He puts the truck in drive and even though I assume we're enroute to either a hotel or an all-night wedding chapel, I don't bother to ask. But he still tells me.

"We're heading out to my father's beach house. It's a beautiful place," he says. *So*, I re-phrase it to myself, *we're going to a free hotel.* I try to play it cool inside my head, but the thoughts of what will probably happen at his father's beach house, keeps scurrying through my mind, their sharp claws digging into my growing anxiety. It doesn't matter how good-looking Oscar is, he just looks like a rapist to me now. I stay frozen on my seat.

"You don't talk much," Oscar says, when we've driven far enough that I don't recognize anything anymore. The suburbs are fading to countryside, covered in trees.

"I don't know you," I say. "What's there to talk about?"

"Let's start with the easy stuff. Tell me all your favorites. Colors, movies, food? What do you like?"

"I like to be at home," I tell him. "My favorite is not being married to strangers, and I don't care about movies. I actually know how to read books."

"I like books."

"Books aren't Playboy magazine articles."

"Where did that come from?" he asks. The tone in his voice reminds me that I don't know who he is at all and have no business talking to him like that. I remain frozen, my head twisted toward the window till my neck aches. "Hale, this is going to be a lot harder on both of us if either of us decides not to try, so how about we start again?"

"I don't know what you want from me," I say. Thank God, my voice doesn't crack as I say it, but at least it feels like I've taken the elephant off my shoulders.

"Okay, good, I can answer that," Oscar says. I keep my eyes out the window. "I want you to be a loyal wife. I want you to cook for me, and keep up our house, and I want you to be good in bed."

There is a playful smirk in his tone. I almost gag.

"You're a pig," I say. I don't care if he shoves me out of the moving vehicle. He just laughs.

"Because I want you to be good in bed? That's a problem?" He laughs again. "Don't you want that from me?"

"I don't want anything from you," my voice cracks this time, a big jagged crack right down the middle. Oscar's laugh suddenly cuts off.

"Wait," he says and all I can think is *here it comes.* And I'm not wrong. "Have you ever been with a man before?"

When I don't answer him, he clears his throat.

"My favorite author is Steinbeck," he begins softly.

#

Oscar fills up the silence by telling me things about himself. He loves movies, especially comedies, and he tells me he was vegan for a week, but it didn't work out. He says that although he doesn't own any shirts or cars, or even a room in his house that is yellow, it is still his favorite color. I don't want to care, but I listen to every word he says, because his voice soothes me somehow. When he tells me about the music he likes, he turns on the radio and, eventually, it takes over the whole conversation. I'm almost disappointed when he stops talking, but I finally lean my head against the headrest, close my eyes, and drift off to the sound of a nightclub piano.

"Hale?"

There's a hand on my arm, a voice I don't recognize, and a truck all around me when I jolt back to consciousness.

"Whoa, hey, we're here." Oscar's voice is still all mellow and soft. I fell asleep, but now I feel more exhausted than refreshed, and more freaked out than not. I rub my eyes and look out the window to see the place he was talking about.

While I wondered if Oscar's beach house would be a mansion on stilts in the sand, it isn't. Instead, it is a cute little bungalow set into a clearing in the woods. There are no streetlights, but a floodlight on the screened-in, front porch illuminates the entrance. When I step out of the truck, I can hear the waves somewhere close, licking the shore.

"Come on in," Oscar says, walking past me with most of our bags slung across his shoulders. I follow behind him, through the screened porch that smells a little musty and into the cabin. And I immediately feel like I'm at home in the kind of home I've never had, but the one that would make everyone feel at home, no matter who they were or where they came from.

There is a braided oval rug on the floor, a rocking chair, an easy chair, and a couch. The walls are gray-blue slats; the ceiling and trim are white. A staircase leads upstairs, but there is a turn at a landing, so all I see is the wall. To the right is a bathroom door and, to the left, the kitchen. It is a rectangle space with an old stove and a double washtub instead of a regular sink.

Running across the ends of both the living room and kitchen, is an entire wall of windows, with a windowed door at the kitchen end. A dining room table is stretched across the middle, overlooking the dark shadows outside. Oscar flips a switch and exterior floodlights illuminate a sandy shore only a few yards away. I can make out the ripple of the waves lapping up onto the sand.

Oscar puts down our bags and comes to stand beside me.

"What do you think?" he asks, and I'm suddenly even more aware of him than before. He's a little taller than me, and his body seems to be sending radioactive waves right through me. I tingle beside him and flex my fingers to make it stop. I try to flex *everything* to make it stop, but the fizzy tingle slips lower in my stomach.

"It's a nice place," I say. It sounds absolutely stupid. A place like this, where you can walk in and feel like you've belonged here all your life, is not a 'nice' place. But this place also belongs to Oscar and his father, who both expect me to agree to give up my life in order to bury their mistake. I quiver with the tingles and Oscar blows out a small laugh.

"Cold?" he asks.

"No." I say.

"There's probably nothing to eat in here. We'll have to grab some things tomorrow in town. But if you're tired, there's a bed upstairs."

I'm exhausted, but I don't know what he means by 'a bed'. Does he mean there's only one? Of course, he has to; he must be. He might still think we're getting married, but even worse, he knows I'm stuck out here in the woods with him. I force my brain to stay alert. I walk over to the couch and sit down, but it doesn't help me to stay alert when the cushion is so incredibly soft that it feels like I'm drifting in the soft palm of God. My eyes flutter shut, but I force them back open just as Oscar turns around.

"I'll grab everything out of the truck," he says and I nod, but the minute he steps out the door, I can't keep my eyes open one moment longer. Not one.

His arm is sliding beneath me and, for a second, I actually think I am little again and my father is scooping me up for bed. He pulls me to him and then a scent hits me that fires off alert centers in my brain. Sandalwood. Apples. Sandalwood. Apples. My father never smelled like sandalwood or apples. I scramble to place it as my eyes pop open, and my mouth follows right behind. I scream in Oscar's face, and he dumps me back down on the cushions. I scuttle up the arm.

"It's me!" he shouts. "My God, I think you blew my ear drum!"

"Don't touch me then!"

"I was going to put you up in bed, so you wouldn't wake up with a crick in your neck!"

"Maybe I want a crick in my neck!" I shriek. Oscar throws up his hands, like he's trying to show God that he tried. He's given it his all and I'm impossible.

"There's a bed upstairs, if you want it," he says. He crosses the room to the sunroom door that leads outside and I'm a little surprised when he doesn't slam the door after letting himself out.

I get off the couch and stand in center of the little cabin living room, unsure of where to go or what to do next. My bags aren't on the floor anymore. I bet he took them upstairs. Another squinty stare out the sunroom windows and I can make out Oscar's shape, moving down to the water's edge, so I decide to creep my way up the stairs and find my things.

The staircase is narrow and the steps are steep. I can only put the balls of my feet on them to climb, and I hold tightly to the railing. At the top, there is a wide open door. The landing leads into a huge room. I feel for a light switch inside the doorway, but when I flip it up, the room is only cast with the flicker of fake candles plugged in on each side of the bed, and the light makes the room jump with shadows. I step back, clinging to the rail and ready to run, until I realize the shadows are cast from the swaying trees outside. I creep over to the foot of the bed where my bags and Oscar's are heaped together on the floor. I peer out of the enormous window that overlooks the inland lake outside. The thick curtains, that should probably be drawn shut, are tied back at either side of the window. I try to see Oscar down below, but it is too dark.

There are two matching dressers against the opposite walls, and a wicker chair with fluffy cushions pointed toward the sprawling bed that takes up the middle of the room. The bed has huge, wood balls at each corner and, when my eyes travel upward, I see a skylight surrounded by mirror tiles on the ceiling.

Oh my God. This is obviously not a bed for sleeping. The thought of Oscar, or Mr. Maree, being here, doing *those things*, makes the shaking tree shadows suddenly look like ghosts of women dancing around the edges of the bed. My stomach turns and I spin on my heel, grabbing two of my bags, to retreat down the stairs, but run flat into Oscar's chest.   The impact knocks me backward, but Oscar grabs my upper arms so I don't fall right on my rear end.

"You okay?" he asks. Of course I'm not, and I don't know when I'll ever be okay again, but his hands, curled around my arms, send the radioactive waves right through me. As if I need that. The ghost women dance around us like they're doing voodoo, throwing their thin arms, and swaying their leaves. The glinting candlelight catches in both Oscar's eyes and the mirrors overhead. Without any warning, the room fills up with a milky glow, as the clouds move away from the moon overhead.

"Come and lay down with me," he says. I stand there, like a scarecrow, as he walks away. He sits, kicks up his feet on top of the covers and lies back with his arms folded behind his head.

"It's okay," he says, flicking his eyes to the unwrinkled, emptiness beside him. "I'm not going to lay a finger on you. I promise. Get under the covers if you want. I'll stay on top. Just come talk to me."

I don't. I'm not that stupid. Instead, I move along the outskirts of the room and take a seat in the catcher's-mitt-shaped wicker chair. It creaks and snaps as I sit down, and the voodoo ghost women flail their arms before they finally settle down too.

"What do you want to tell me?" I ask.

"Nothing," he says. He keeps his eyes on the ceiling. "I spent the ride up here telling you about me. But now I want to hear about you."

"I want to talk about Sophia," I say.

The hint of a frown streaks across his profile before he asks, "What about her?"

"Aren't you mad? Aren't you flipped out over what happened?"

"Of course I am," he says. "I'm mad as hell. I didn't even know she was cheating on me until the guy confronted my dad. And now the guy is dead. I'm completely flipped out about the entire thing. That's why we're here."

"But you talked to her."

"I did. Today." He finally takes his eyes off the ceiling and stares at me from the bed. It gives me an unsettled feeling, like a moth spotted in a room. "She acted like nothing happened. She might not have heard yet. All she wanted to do was make plans for Landon's birthday. It made me sick to know that she would act like everything was good between us, when she'd been with someone else."

"Why would she send him after you?"

"No idea. I've already told you this. I don't know anything, except that he showed up at the bar and didn't recognize that my dad wasn't me."

I want to believe him. The clouds drift over the moon, darkening the room, but his eyes are still on me. The voodoo tree ghosts wave their arms in dramatic bursts, but then grow still, and it's just Oscar and me in this bedroom, alone again, looking at one another in the flickering, fake candlelight. I want to believe every word, and make this whole crazy mess feel logical, or even just possible, but I can't. This whole thing is dangerous and stupid.

"If the cops find out what happened, it won't make any difference if we're married. In fact, it'll look worse. It'll look exactly like what it is: a cover up."

Oscar rolls off the bed and onto his feet. He glides toward me like smoke, and I press my back into the chair, as he moves closer.

"You're my alibi, Hale," he says. He drops down on his knees in front of me, so that we are looking at each other at eye level. "This is a marriage of convenience for both of us. My family has lots of money. Whatever you want, I can probably get it for you. My dad's already setting your father up with a good business.

"And you've got the ability to be my father's alibi, Hale. You and your father can clear my father's name. All you have to do is be the girl I've been in love with. Marry me. It would be proof to the world that my father and your father had already gone home together before it all happened. If we said we were hanging out at your house that night. We could be their alibi. They could look forever for the other drunk who did a hit-and-run on Tatum. That stuff happens. It's not wrong, what I'm asking you to do. I'm just asking you to stop an innocent man from losing everything over something that wasn't even his fault. No one meant to hurt anyone, but the accident happened and it could end up hurting all of us. Unless we do this the right way, and then no one gets hurt. It's a good deal, Hale. You should take it."

"So, if it's a marriage of convenience, than we don't really have to be...*technically* married to each other," I say. His eyes are so steady that they make me feel like I'm rippling. "You could have girlfriends, and I wouldn't have to...we wouldn't have to, you know, live together, like married people."

Oscar reaches out, sliding his fingertips softly over my knee.

"That wouldn't work," he says. "This isn't how I ever expected to find a wife either, but it is what it is. We need to be able to trust each other completely. I don't see how either of us could do that, if we were dating other people and just living a lie. I'm for real, Hale. I know you're nervous, but way back in my family history, there were lots of arranged marriages, and they worked. If both people want to be married to one another, if they really believe in making it work, they can be happy."

"I don't know what to say," I tell him. I feel the gentle pressure of his fingers on my knee.

"Say yes," he says.

"You're a stranger."

"But I don't have to be," he says. His fingers slip up my leg and I tense. He whispers, "Don't be afraid of me, okay?"

I'm scared all the way from one end to the other as his fingers move up to my thigh. All my thoughts spin and collide in my head like asteroids. I want my dad to have a chance. I want him to get off welfare. I don't want to be trapped all my life by poverty either. Maybe this is the way out.

But I don't know who this man is, that is kneeling in front of me, sending shock waves through me with his touch. I keep glancing away, but every time I look back, his gaze is still there, intense and rooted and somehow, gentle. I'm starting to feel all Munchausen. How can I just do this in this strange house, in this strange room, with this stranger, even if I do know he likes Steinbeck and the color yellow?

But what difference does it really make? So what if I get married or have my first time here? I'm eighteen. His eyes are so deep; I want to climb into them and hide from all of this. Why do I need to stay a virgin? Why not just make the jump? His touch slides under the frayed edge of my shorts and the tingling inside me goes into overdrive.

"Mmm." His eyes close with the sound he makes.

"This isn't right," I tell him.

"Sure it is," he murmurs. "This is what married people do..."

His fingertip crests the inside of my thigh and as many tingles as there are, the absolute fear of what he means to do with me sends a cold, hard shake all the way into the very middle of my gut. I pull his hand away and am surprised at how easily he lets me do it.

"I don't know you, and we're not married people," I say. He sits back and gives me a closed-mouth grin. It's an *okay, not this time* kind of grin that is even more unsettling than the quiver of ice cold fear I had a moment ago. The grin scares me most because, while it says *not this time*, it also says, as clear as day, *next time.*

CHAPTER FIVE

OSCAR SAID HE WOULD SLEEP downstairs, but when I wake up and roll over in the morning, my face smashes up against his bare back. I skitter backward, right off the bed and Oscar rolls over, rubbing his eyes. He's still got his pants on, but no shirt, no shoes and, as I stare at his bare chest, all I can think is that his chest looks like it has been totally serviced. I could probably bounce a quarter off any muscle between his neck and belly button. Oscar smirks at me and stretches as he sits up.

"That wasn't so bad, was it? Our first time sleeping together," he says. Another smirk from over his shoulder. His back is as solid as his front, for God's sake. It twangs a cord of desire between my legs that vibrates a strong note of panic right into my stomach and makes my heart race. Oscar wouldn't have any problem holding me down if he wanted to. I wonder if that's why he's half naked; he wants me to know who's really got the upper hand here.

"Virgin humor," I say sourly. "That's really funny."

That wipes the smirk off his face. He stands up and goes to one of his bags. The sun shines through the window and his skin is so smooth and tan in the light, it appears nearly edible. I look away.

"I just meant that you don't have to worry about sleeping beside me. You need to be fine with it, because there's only one bed, and I'm not sleeping on the couch."

"I can," I say, but I feel the twinge of regret over not being able to wake up in this gorgeous bed with the sun reaching through the skylight to warm the sheets. Or maybe it was Oscar warming the sheets.

I shouldn't feel any regret about not waking up beside him, but a tiny, dirty little part of me does. I've always been one of those girls who practiced abstinence, and preached its benefits to my choirgirl, Sher, but we both knew that our virginity wasn't always intact because we wanted it that way.

But we knew we *should*. Sher's mother beat it into our heads, usually with an arm wave to their overly-child-packed apartment and the advice, "Don't get knocked up, girls. You see what happens? You get to work three jobs, and you'll still never have enough. Or you'll die from a sex disease. Or, at the very least, everyone will think you're a whore. Do yourselves a favor and keep your legs shut."

Sher and I repeatedly told each other how smart we were for never screwing around, but we also talked at great length about how we thought it all worked, how we thought we would do it, who we'd do it with, and how much we wanted it to happen. And, at night, I couldn't help that, sometimes, I'd think about the way a guy looked at me at school, or I'd read a hot scene in one of the romance books, and my fingers would meet up with my desire in the dark. I'd fantasize that it was someone else's fingers inside me and it would feel like fireworks when I came, but once I was done, I'd always feel guilty and ashamed for having done it at all. I knew this was how I was supposed to feel, because my dad, and Sher's mom, and TV church broadcasts on Sunday mornings, kept saying that girls were never supposed to want to do that kind of thing with themselves, or with anyone else. When I'd admitted it to Sher once, she just laughed her squealy, high-pitched, nervous laugh and said, *Oh my God!* But she never actually said that she did it too, or that she had that same kind of intense *urge* like I did.

Now, looking at Oscar's half-naked body, that deep urge tugs at me again and I'm ashamed that it's there at all. Even if I think about marrying Oscar, it doesn't make the urge feel okay. I just feel like I should never, ever want to do what my body seems to be screaming for me to do. And then, on top of the guilt, I feel like an enormous loser prude.

"What are you thinking about?" Oscar asks, as he takes fresh clothes from his bag. No way am I telling him any of *that*.

"I was thinking I should go home today."

He pauses. "Hale, you have to stop with that." Then he jumps subjects. "We've got to get some food for around here and, if there's anything you need, make a list."

"How long are you expecting to stay out here?"

"Probably a couple of weeks. However long it takes for you to trust me."

"What you mean is: until I say 'yes' to marriage."

"Pretty much." He smiles at me.

"How can you act like this is all normal?" I say.

"Because it has to be," he says simply. "Arranged marriages work. We just have to get used to each other."

"That's really optimistic," I say. "So, it wouldn't matter to you who you had to marry to get your dad out of trouble?"

Oscar tosses his clothes on the bed and steps in close to me. We're only standing a foot apart and I can feel the heat radiating off his skin.

"If my dad was in trouble and I had to get with a toad, well then, it's a pretty sure bet that I'd get with a toad because, and you'll see this over time, the Maree family is as loyal to one another as they come. But," he says, moving in so close that my nose is nearly touching his chest and the smell of apples and sandalwood fill every breath I take, "I got incredibly lucky that I didn't have to take a toad for the team. In fact, if you are half as much on the inside as you are on the outside, Hale, than I didn't even have to dodge a bullet. What I did was hit the mother of all jackpots."

He stands there a minute, making me sway under the compliments, and his scent, and his closeness. Then he leans over me, brushing up against me as he grabs his clothes.

"I'm going to grab a shower," he says. "I'll try to leave you some hot water."

#

He's on the phone when I emerge from the bathroom, my teeth chattering. Despite his quick shower, the hot water ran out half way through mine. I throw on a pair of jeans and a long sleeve white tee, and they stick to me, but I thank God again that my father actually threw some of the clothes I like into my bags.

I don't sit with him at the table. His conversation never pauses, but his eyes follow me to the chair near the wall of windows. The sun shines in, and the chair is warm as I brush out my hair. I put my back to Oscar, and I can't help but hear every word of his conversation.

"You can come up and meet her, sure...You're bringing Amy? So, you guys are making it work, huh? Yeah, but I don't know if it's a good idea...they're best friends...What do you *think* she's going to do? Ok, yeah, ok...we'll see you then."

I hear him click off his phone and set it down on the table. I keep brushing my hair, even as the chair grits across the floor and his footsteps tread toward me. I think he's going to put his hands on my shoulders, or lean down and try to kiss my neck. As I think of all the things he could do, and how it might feel so shamefully good in the warm sunlight, he walks past me instead.

"Ready to go?" he asks.

"Go where?"

"Town. We need food. Aren't you hungry?" he asks. I just nod. I feel so stupidly helpless without money, a car, or even a phone. I've got no way to take care of myself right now besides trusting him to do it for me. Part of me wants to kick him in the nuts and steal his truck. The other part knows that, even if I had his truck, there'd be nowhere for me to really go. So,I get on my shoes, even though I feel as though I'm moving like a tin man.

Outside, the air really hits me. It's colder than I expect and it smells cleaner than I'm used to. I can hear the water rippling up to the shore as we get into the truck, and it seems like I should be happy instead of still so tense. Oscar must see it too, because he starts talking.

"My friend, Landon, is coming up on Friday," he says. Two days from now. Then, with a little less enthusiasm, "He's bringing Amy, his new girlfriend too."

"Isn't it going to be create a total train wreck that I'm here?" I say, as Oscar puts his arm over the back of my seat to back up the truck. Something about it feels intimate, like I'm in his arms, even though I'm really only at his fingertips. I press my back to the edge of the seat. "Sophia doesn't even know about me yet, does she?"

"No. But Landon won't bat an eye. He's the closest friend I've got, and he never liked Sophia much anyway. But he's also with Amy. That could be more of a problem."

"Didn't you say on the phone that Sophia and Amy are best friends?"

"I did," he says, removing his arm from the back of my seat. He puts the truck in drive and steers us down the winding dirt drive back to the paved, main road. The Marees seem to have a thing for long, obscured driveways, and this one is beautiful. The trees stretch up along the sides and nearly touch overhead, like a cathedral ceiling. "I'll have to call Sophia today and tell her I'm leaving her for you."

"Great," I grumble. "I get to be the bitch that took you away from your girlfriend."

"No," he corrects me softly. "What I'll tell her is that you are the girl I couldn't resist. You are the girl that I met by chance, because our fathers were doing business together, and I fell in love with you at first sight. I was the one that pursued you, even though I had a girlfriend at the time. I couldn't help myself. I'll tell her you were never the *other* woman, Hale, because you are *the one*."

When he stops talking, I realize I'm leaning a little off my seat with my mouth open. The way he looks at me is so intense, even just the fleeting glance he takes from the road to give to me, throws me off-guard and it takes me a moment to remember that this whole thing is just a cover up. But, if he can say it again the way he just did, making me forget that he's not really in love with me, than I'm sure his friends won't have any trouble believing the lie either.

"Yeah, stick with that," I say, settling back against the seat. "It sounds real."

"It should," he says, but he keeps his eyes on the road and his jaw seems to harden a little. "We need to be on the same page."

"Your page has a wedding certificate on it though."

"So should yours."

"No," I wiggle in the seat. "Mine has more of a note on it."

That gets me a glance with a cocked eyebrow attached to it.

"A note?" he asks.

"Like a *would you like to date me* note."

"Oh," he says and closes his mouth with a thoughtful *hmm*. It takes a second before he continues, "I'll tell you what. Let's consider this a date. We're going to be at the beach house for a while, so let's think of this as one long, uninterrupted date."

"But dating doesn't mean we'll end up together."

"I think we both realize that this date has to end exactly like that," he says solidly. "But we don't have to make anything official overnight either. I don't have any problem with you taking some time to get comfortable with me."

It's as much breathing space as I'm going to get out of him, I think.

"And you can get comfortable with me too," I say.

"No need," he says. "I was comfortable with you from the first moment I met you." His glance jumps from the road, and washes over me in static waves that make my heart blink a beat before he looks away.

#

"What do you like to eat?" he asks as we pull up in front of a grocery store. 'Town' is a strip of individual buildings that house all the necessary stores: a grocery, a gas station, a hardware and a rickety brown building with a hand-painted sign that says:

COME IN ITALIANS FOOD

"Not Italians. I don't eat them," I say pointing to the sign, and he laughs.

While we walk through the aisles of the grocery store, I try to decipher things about Oscar by what he puts in the cart. He likes pickles- two jars of kosher spears- and he buys expensive coffee. He gets eggs, milk and bread (snore) and fruit, chicken, steak, hamburger with buns and lunchmeat (snore more). He throws in peanut butter and a few bagged salads, bottled water, champagne, beer, dressing and carrots...the list keeps going and the cart is piled like we'll never see civilization again.

I'm not a detective after all. The only thing that the grocery cart says about Oscar is that he doesn't know what he's doing, because he's buying way too much of everything. It would probably cost him less to have the entire store relocated onto the front lawn of the cabin.

He pays the bill, while I hold a teetering cake in place, so it doesn't plop out onto the floor.

"You really think we're going to eat all of this?" I ask, as he grabs the cart handle and pushes our mammoth pile slowly enough that I can still hold onto the cake and manage the three bags of chips that want to slide off the top of Mt. Grocery.

"I was waiting for you to say what you liked," he says. "You didn't, so I got a little of everything. I'm starving...you like bagels?"

I nod. We heave everything into the truck, stacking and smashing it all, so we can make it fit. Oscar hands me the cake and a carton of eggs.

"You go ahead and get in. I've got the rest of this," he says. When he finally gets in the truck, he's got two cinnamon bagels with cream cheese on them, and a plastic knife hanging out of his mouth. He flashes me a grin around the knife and hands one of the bagels to me.

With the cake and eggs stacked on my lap for the ride back, I nibble on the bagel and realize that the one thing I've learned about Oscar Maree is that he's trying a lot harder than I am. And I might want to change that.

#

"I'm still hungry, are you?" Oscar says when we've dragged the carload of groceries inside.

"Yes," I say, and the way he smiles makes me feel warm inside. He takes the eggs from the fridge and pulls a skillet from a cupboard.

"Eggs sound good? I can make them however you want, as long as you want them scrambled."

"Seriously?"

"Growing up, my mom always poached them, but I've never been able to do it."

I step up beside him and take the skillet.

"It's just boiling salty water, there's nothing to poaching an egg."

"Unless you're me," he says, stepping aside. I fill the skillet with water, dump in some salt from a shaker on the back of the stove, and set the pan on the oven with a thunk.

"Wait, a minute," I say. "You just want to see if I can cook."

"Maybe I don't want you to see how bad I am at it."

I roll my eyes at him.

"Whatever," I say. "You've got a mother that made poached eggs for you?"

"I had a mother that made eggs. My mom died of breast cancer six years ago."

"Sorry," I tell him, and I mean it. I hear how his voice dips, and I see how he looks away across the floor and out the windows toward the beach. "Is your dad remarried?"

"No," he says. "It's just him and me."

"No brothers or sisters either?"

"Nope. What about you? Siblings?"

I shake my head, watching the tiny bubbles beginning to form in the bottom of the skillet.

"Just me and my dad. My mom's in Texas somewhere, with her new husband and new kids," I say. Oscar winces.

"How long has she been gone?"

"Forever." I shrug, as the skillet bubbles jump up to the top and burst, one after another. I crack an egg into the water. I don't know why I say it, but I tell him, "That's what got my dad drinking."

Oscar steps a little closer, peering into the skillet. I flick water over the eggs so the tops cook too.

"So that's how you do that," he murmurs as if the egg is really interesting. He watches me lift his egg out, drain off the water and slip it into a coffee mug. I hold out the cup to him, but without looking up at me, Oscar adds, "Your dad's been drinking a while then, huh?"

"Yes."

Oscar makes a low rumble in his throat. "I don't drink. You?"

"Yeah right."

"You're a good girl, Hale."

I shoot him a sour glare. "I'm a woman, Oscar."

But the glare doesn't do what I expect. Instead of pushing him away, Oscar moves closer so the eggcup only separates our bodies at waist level.

"Are you now?" Oscar's voice is deep and sultry. I think of a dozen comebacks, but every single one makes me sound like a little kid. With Oscar staring down at me, and the steam of the egg rising up, the room suddenly feels too warm. But I won't let him scare me. I won't look away. Instead, I want to call his bluff and let him know I'm not some little kid he can boss around.

"Kiss me," I say. A smile teases over his lips. He tips his head to one side and squints at me.

"That's what you want now?" he asks. His stare is so intense; I catch my bottom lip in my teeth without even thinking about it. When his eyes flick to my lips, I realize what I'm doing and let go. Oscar smiles. "Why now?"

I don't have an answer, because I didn't expect the question. I thought he'd just give in and kiss me. I didn't expect that he'd resist, or question the direct request. I glance away and take a step back, but Oscar moves forward and grabs my arms.

"Is that what you want?" he asks again, but I can't answer. I don't know. I just want him to see me as an equal, and not some little girl that he can tell what to do. Not a cow. Not even a wife, but a woman who can make up her own mind, and might even be able to make up his, with the right kiss. But my whole plan kind of blows up in my face, because Oscar's not following the script I have in my head. Instead, he's looking at my lips, then drilling into my eyes, and all the womanly wiles I was counting on fail me.

I gulp and push the coffee mug into his gut.

"Never mind," I say. "Here's your egg."

Oscar lets go of my arms, and his hands slide down to take the mug.

"Thanks," he says with a smirk, "for cooking for me."

\#

He won.

He told me before he wanted me to cook for him and I walked right into it. As he turns to get a spoon from the silverware drawer, I walk across the room to the door leading out to the beach. My fingers are on the handle when Oscar says, "Stay and talk to me."

"About what?" I ask with a sigh.

"Anything," he says innocently. "Tell me what you want from me."

"I don't want anything from you."

"You're aiming kind of low, don't you think?" he asks. "Give me something to shoot for. To impress you with. I could be a pretty impressive husband, if I'm motivated."

"Why do we have to keep talking about this stuff? It's boring." I say. Oscar just lifts his spoon to his mouth and takes the first bite of his egg. He closes his eyes and hums, *mmm.*

"You *really* know how to cook," he says. Cooking. That was on his list of what he wanted me to do for him, and it annoys me. So, if he wants something to shoot for, I figure I'll make it impossible.

"I want you to worship me," I say. Oscar's entire forehead wrinkles up with amusement as he chews.

"Worship? Seriously?" he asks, his mouth full.

"Yup."

"You mean like bowing when you walk in the room? Making altars? That kind of thing?"

I roll my eyes. "No. I mean that if I call for you, I want to know that you'll come running. I want to know that, when I walk into a room, you'll notice. That if I burn dinner or turn your t-shirts pink or gain five pounds, you'll still feel lucky to have me. When we talk, I want you to really hear what I'm trying to say. That's what I want from you."

Oscar puts the mug on the counter. I think he's going to tell me I'm a spoiled brat, or that I don't know a thing about how relationships work, but he leans on the counter with one hand and gives me a long stare before he says, "Done."

I drop my fingertips from the door handle.

"I would notice you, Hale," he continues, "if you walked into a room behind a 500 pound lion that was charging straight for me. I would notice you if the room were full of naked women, and I was in deep conversation about my own death. I will always come running, I'll eat the dinner and wear the shirts and I've already thought that if you put on ten more pounds, it'd be a sure bet that I would never let you out of my bed. I've been trying to soak up every word you've said since the first time we spoke, so I think it's only fair that you try just as hard to hear me now. I think you are perfect for me, Hale, and I'm just waiting for you to realize that I'm perfect for you too."

It's like the entire room disappears and all I see is Oscar with his level gaze, as he drops his voice to a whisper and says, "Come here."

But I stay where I am, with the sun warming my back through the windows, and I shake my head at him.

"No," I say. "Come running."

He doesn't hesitate. Oscar crosses the room in four strides, pulling me into his arms. Both of his hands slide up my back, one cupping my head as he brings his mouth down on mine. His lips are softer than I expect. I spin inside his kiss, clinging to him as he pulls my lip between his teeth and gently releases it again. His breath whispers my name across my mouth as he pulls me even closer. With my body crushed against his, and the sunlight from the windows, and his hands sliding down my back, I think I am going to combust.

As his mouth moves against mine again, and his fingers slide over my hips, his cell phone begins to ring. He ignores it, but I pull back.

"Aren't you going to get that?" I ask. He groans, but reaches into his pocket, then steps back, his eyes still boring into mine, and turns on the phone.

"Hello?" His tone could not be more agitated. He listens a moment before his eyes move away from me, out the windows. We're still so close; it feels like an invasion of his privacy to stay there, under his chin, breathing him in, so I back away. His gaze remains far past me.

"Ok...but they still don't have any leads, do they? I thought you said they worked together...well, did Sophia have something to do with it or not?"

He moves then, turning away from me to plant his hand on the edge of the table, his back to me. I follow the arc of his arm, past his broad shoulder, and down to his narrow waist. My skin still tingles where his hands held me steady only a moment ago.

"But he told you Sophia sent him...that they were together...no, it doesn't add up, does it...I don't care what she says. The guy told you he was there because of her, why would he say that if he wasn't? I'll talk to her in a couple days. I'm too confused to say anything right now...Yeah, she's still here with me...I don't know yet, we'll see...alright, well, keep me up on what's going on, okay?...Alright, Dad...yeah, you too...bye."

He switches off the phone and lays it on the table.

"What's going on?" I ask. He shakes his head, and rubs his eyes with one hand.

"We don't know," he says. "Sophia's either excellent at playing dumb, or she really doesn't know who Rick Tatum is. She's been blowing up my house phone trying to get me."

"Why doesn't she call your cell?"

"She doesn't have this number," he says. He's still looking out to the beach. "The only ones that do are my father and Landon."

"Are you going to call her?"

"When I figure out what to say to her, I will. She was cheating on me, Hale. I don't think she needs to be told that it's over."

"What if you're wrong?" I ask. What I mean is, *if she didn't have anything to do with this, are you going back to her?* I don't know why it is such a dark question that I have a problem asking it. I shouldn't care. It's just getting really hard to remember that Oscar's a complete stranger.

"The guy knew her name," he says. "I'm pretty sure she had everything to do with it. Look, I'm going to go for a walk and clear my head."

And that's it. He goes out and the door latches shut behind him with a gritty bang.

"Come running," I whisper, but he doesn't hear me.

CHAPTER SIX

HE IS GONE FOR TOO LONG. I finally follow his path out the sunroom door and down the short, curved sandy path to the beach. The trees open up and the lake stretches out even larger than I thought. I'm surprised that, although I can see the other side, there are no houses looking back. The only sign of life I see is Oscar sitting at the end of a long dock with his feet in the water. I pick my way around a beached, aluminum boat, but I only get a foot away from shore before I stop. The wobble of the boards makes Oscar twist around to see me.

"Hi," he says, scooting himself, and his removed shoes, over to make a spot for me. "You want to come sit?"

"No," I say, backing off the dock. The slight quake in the structure makes me feel lightheaded, but it's the thought of falling in the water that fills me with sharp icicles.

"Come on, the view's even better out here."

"That's okay," I say, but he's on his feet already, walking down the dock to me. When he gets to the end, he steps off and says, "Are you mad about something?"

"No," I say, but Oscar starts explaining himself anyway.

"Sorry that I walked out of there like that. I was just surprised and needed a minute to think. The guy that died, Rick Tatum - my dad doesn't think Sophia even knew him, but Tatum told my dad that Sophia sent him. It doesn't make sense. Tatum thought my dad was me, and told him to stop dating Sophia, because Tatum said he'd been seeing her the last couple weeks. But I guess Sophia's trying to find me, and keeps calling the house and begging my dad to tell her where I'm at. I can't figure out why she would do that, if her other boyfriend was just found dead behind a bar. She'd have to know. It was on the news. Unless she just didn't see it. My dad said it was just a short blurb, but Sophia would've wanted to hear what happened from Tatum, if she actually sent him. My dad said that if she knows anything, she's totally convincing him in the opposite direction."

"Maybe you should just call her," I say. I don't say it very loud.

"I can't," he says, rubbing his temple. "I still don't know what happened yet. I don't want to say anything to her before I know exactly what's going on."

I wonder what he'll end up saying, if she didn't have anything to do with it. I wonder if he'll say he wants her back, and I wonder what that will mean to me.

"You want to come sit on the dock? Put your feet in the water?" He grabs my hand, warm and soft, and a shot of jealousy about Sophia shoots through me. He steps onto the dock. I pull my hand back, but he doesn't let go. "What's the matter?"

"I, uh, I don't know how to swim," I say.

"Ohhh," he breathes, but instead of letting go, he squeezes my hand. "You can still sit on the dock though."

"No," I feel the color drain from my face. My breathing accelerates and piles up in my throat. "It freaks me out. If I'm out there and I fall in, it's too deep."

Oscar looks out at the end of the dock. "It's shallow up here, but see that red beam way down there? The one with the red stripe at the top?" I spot the beam immediately. There's a few yellow-tipped ones before it, and then, about thirty feet away, at the halfway point on the dock, there is a bright red beam. "That's where the drop-off starts. But up here, it's shallow. The deepest it gets is up to your thighs. If you fell in, all you'd have to do is stand up."

He gives my hand a little tug, but I pull back.

"No, I think I'll stay here."

"Come with me. You can see down to the bottom. It's all rippled sand."

"No thanks."

"I'll be sure you don't fall in."

"Nuh uh," I shake my head, but he doesn't give up.

"How about just coming in up to your calves? You can do that, can't you?" he asks, as he wades onto the abbreviated beach. I remove my shoes and follow him in, a little embarrassed.

"Yes, I can do that," I say, but when he pulls me a little further, the sloshing that rises up over my knees is reflected in my belly, and I have to put on the brakes again. I feel myself going pale. Oscar turns back to me and ducks his head to catch my gaze.

"Too much?" he asks. I nod stiffly. "Let's sit down."

"Not in the water," I say, but Oscar's expression tells me that I must look as scared as I feel.

"Don't worry about getting wet. We've got dry clothes up at the house." He kneels down in the water, tugging me down with him, but I stumble forward and end up on my hands and knees. I yelp and panic and hold my chin up out of the water. The idea of it on my face, going down my nose or into my mouth makes me want to throw up. Oscar gets hold of me and hauls me up, onto my knees.

"You're okay," he tries to assure me. The entire front of my shirt is soaked, and my entire body starts to tremor. The wet fabric is as miserable as holding a frozen, metal cookie sheet against my skin, but worse than anything – I can't catch my breath. Oscar stands up, pulling me with him, and wraps an arm around my waist. "You really don't like the water," he tries to joke. My lips are quivering too much to answer.

The sand sticks to my feet as Oscar guides me back to the cabin door. Once we're inside, he only lets go of me when I'm planted on a kitchen chair. He's gone for a moment, while I hiccup my breaths, and returns with a fluffy blue towel from the bathroom. He puts it around my shoulders, and I don't remember anything else until I open my eyes again.

#

"Hale?"

I'm lying on the couch and Oscar is hovering over me, tapping my cheek. When my eyes open, Oscar lets out a breath and says, "Oh, thank God. You scared me to death."

"What?" I say, and then, I remember the water and look down. My shirt is missing. So are my shorts. I'm just lying there in my bra and panties with a towel bunched up beside me. I grab it as I sit up, trying to cover myself. I spot my shorts and shirt in a soggy heap on the floor. I gape at Oscar. "You *undressed* me?"

For whatever reason, my words startle him. He takes a step back, glancing at the clothes and me and runs a hand through his hair. "No...I mean, yes, I did, but...no." he stammers. "It's not what you're thinking. Not at all. You passed out and I thought the wet clothes were doing it..."

"My clothes?" I glare at him. "You think it was my clothes, and not that you pulled me into the water after I told you I'm *fucking afraid* of it?"

The towel doesn't cover anything and it keeps slipping. But Oscar's not looking at my body. He's combing his fingers over his face, frustrated.

"I thought it'd calm you down," he says.

"Dunking me, or undressing me?" I ask.

"Both, actually."

"Bad call," I tell him, getting off the couch. When he looks back at me, his eyes slide down my body, and I shout at him, "QUIT LOOKING AT ME!"

I slip past him and scramble up the stairs, but Oscar's right behind me.

"Hale," he says, but I don't stop to listen to him. I'm all the way to our bags, still heaped on the floor, before he says my name again. I ignore his pleading tone and rifle my bag for the first shirt and shorts I can find. Oscar stands two feet away, watching me as I yank on a shirt and step into my shorts, my cheeks hot. From my peripheral vision, I can tell he hasn't looked away once, but I keep my eyes on the floor, even after I'm completely dressed again.

"I was just trying to help you get over your fear," he says softly.

"That's not the way. Don't help me like that again."

"I won't," he says. "Not until you ask me to."

"Oh, I won't ask," I snap, but instead of turning and leaving like I think he should, Oscar steps closer to me.

"You're right," he says and his smirk is back. "You won't ask. So, I'll promise you this: I won't, until you beg me. Fair enough?"

Before I can answer him, he turns away and goes down the stairs, without looking back.

\#

I stay upstairs, crunched into the catcher's mitt chair, unsure of what to do. Oscar moves around downstairs and even though he's not slamming doors or banging cupboards – in fact, everything sounds pretty peaceful, as if he's being careful not to wake me or something – I still have to assume he's angry. When I think of it, I made a huge deal out of nothing. It's not like I was naked. The thought of being naked in front of Oscar makes my mind wander, until I feel tingles running all through me.

Someone knocks on the door downstairs. My thoughts quickly refocus on Oscar's footsteps treading across the living room to the front door.

"Hey!" his voice is excited, welcoming. "What are you doing here? I thought you weren't coming up until Friday! Come on in!"

The door creaks wide open, and I hear the thunk of suitcases banging against the door frame and a syrupy female voice say, "What's going on with you, Oscar? Soph's been worried sick about you!"

"Good to see you, Amy," Oscar says, but his voice is tight. Amy and Landon. Landon, Oscar's best friend and Amy, Sophia's bestie. I'm so screwed.

"You up here by yourself?" Landon's voice wanders, as if he's craning his neck to look around.

"No, actually," Oscar says. "I'm not."

"What do you mean?" Amy's tone is sharp now. "Soph's home right now."

"Obviously, it's not Sophia," Landon says, as if it's all a good joke. A game. "Where is she? It is a *she*, isn't it?"

"Very funny," Oscar says. "Her name's Hale and she's upstairs."

"Hale?" Amy's voice splits the pause like a hunting knife. "What are you talking about, Oscar? You're still dating Sophia, Mr. Faithful. At least, as far as she knows. You just went missing, and you haven't even bothered to tell her that it's because you're seeing someone else? Do you know how asshole-ish that is?"

"Quit busting his balls," Landon says.

"Why shouldn't I?"

"Because it's none of our business, hon."

"My best friend's boyfriend snuck away to be with some other girl, *hon*. I think that makes it my business."

"No." Oscar's polite grin is obvious in the way his words turn up. "Land's right. I appreciate the concern, but it's not your business."

There is a long pause and a sigh.

"She's my friend," Amy says, but her tone throws up its hands in surrender. "At least call her and tell her what's going on, so I don't get in trouble for knowing. And bring down your new one."

"Don't call her that," Oscar says. "Her name is Hale."

"So you *are* playing the field," Amy's voice shoots up in the middle of the word. "I thought you weren't looking to do anymore of that?"

"I wasn't, but this girl slammed it out of the park," Oscar says. And then, as if to stop Amy, he says, "You guys wanna meet her?"

And that's when I start feeling like I should've been prying the window open about ten minutes ago.

CHAPTER SEVEN

"HALE," OSCAR CALLS FROM THE bottom of the stairs. I don't want to answer. I think of every excuse, that I'm sleeping, or sick, or even passed out again, but all it will do is bring them up here.

"Is there really somebody up there?" Amy asks. But by then, I've moved across the room to the stairs, and the top step creaks when I step down on it. Amy goes silent, while each step decides to whisper a squeak as I come down. By the time I reach the bottom, it seems like the stairs have silenced everyone.

Oscar is waiting with a grin. Landon gives me a curious, but welcoming, smile. And Amy, a girl with a natural slope to her eyebrows that makes her look angry, actually stands there with no expression. Her mouth hangs a tiny bit, and her eyes are so bland that they appear almost sorrowful as she takes me in.

"This is Hale," Oscar says, stepping in front of Amy and reaching for my hand. I guess it's time to really sell the charade, but I blush a little when I spot my clothes still in a heap near the couch. Amy's eyes dart after mine and she sees them too. I wonder what Oscar's friends would think if they knew that, a half hour ago, I wasn't slipping out of those clothes on my own, and that I wasn't even coherent when Oscar did it for me.

"I'm Landon," Landon says, juggling all the bags hanging off him, with his hand out. He gives my hand a shake so quick that it could snap me like a towel, if he'd used the full-range of my arm. Landon's a thick, blond monster with cargo shorts, and hair that is carefully spiked on top. He says, "Good to meet you."

He seems to mean it, just like Oscar said he would.

"And this is Amy," Oscar says, when Amy doesn't introduce herself first. Besides the eyebrows, Amy is a tall, blond Popsicle stick of a woman with a long nose and beautiful curls. She puts on a grin and reaches for my hand, doing a light fingertip-to-fingertip shake, gone before it was really ever there. She turns to Oscar.

"Should we just haul everything upstairs, honey?" she asks. Something in her *honey* drizzles a little too warmly. I don't know why, but I wrap my arms around Oscar's waist and tell myself I'm just doing it for the show. I feel oddly good about wanting to convince Amy that Oscar is mine and our relationship is real.

"You're okay with sharing our bed?" I ask, looking up into his eyes. I let the rest of the thought trail away. Oscar's eyes flash devilishly before he ducks down and kisses my forehead, as if he's done it every day for years.

"No, I'm not," he says. "We'll put the inflato-bed down here, if that's good with you, Land?"

"I can sleep any place," Landon shrugs, letting all the bags finally fall off his shoulders and onto the floor. He leans over to kiss Amy's cheek, even though she's still staring at me. Her expression makes her look like a statue in a wax museum. She sways from the peck on her cheeks, and snaps out of her stare in time to catch Oscar's eye, then turns to plant a kiss on Landon. She open-mouths it. Landon's body goes rigid a second with surprise. Oscar and I exchange an uncomfortable glance.

Amy comes up for air and, looking back at Oscar, says, "It's fine. I can sleep any place too."

#

"Your friends are really weird," I whisper to Oscar. He's lying on our bed, and I'm sitting beside him. We'd retreated upstairs after Landon and Amy had blown up the inflato-mattress near the front windows. When they laid down on it, and started touching each other's hair and giggling softly, Oscar suggested that he and I go upstairs to give them their privacy. I was happy to escape the two of them, especially Amy and the glares she kept shooting at me.

"Not Landon," Oscar whispers back. "He's the best guy you'll ever meet, but Amy...yeah, she's weird sometimes."

"She's just looking out for her friend," I say darkly. "I can't blame her for that. Sher would do the same for me."

I stare at his phone on the nightstand and I think of Sher.

"Can I use your phone?" I ask.

"You want to call your dad?"

"No, my friend, Sher." I say. I'll never want to call my dad. Not anytime soon, at least. Oscar thinks on it for a minute.

"What are you going to say to her exactly?"

"I don't know. Why?"

"Are you going to say you're trapped at some guy's beach house?" I see the nervousness when he says it. He's trying to act like he's kidding, but he's not.

"No," I say, although it had occurred to me. "I was going to tell her that I was kidnapped by a dude that is forcing me to marry him."

"Forcing? No, that wouldn't attract any attention," he says. "Sorry, I think my phone is out of order."

"Come on," I say. "I was just kidding. I was going to tell her I was at my cousin's house."

Oscar sits up, his chest touching my shoulder, the side of his leg touching my back. His raw energy crashes right through me in waves. My body comes alive, prickling as if it's waking from a ten-year sleep. The stinging tickle centers itself between my legs.

"You want to use my phone?" he asks. His breath is on my cheek. "I'll let you."

But as I reach for the phone, Oscar grabs my hand.

"For a kiss," he says. I try to pull my hand away, but he doesn't let go.

"Forget it, ya perv," I say.

"What's the problem? You've already kissed me once. I think it's fair to say you enjoyed it." He draws back my hair over my shoulder. "But I'm not even asking for a kiss *from you*. I'll tell you what – I'll give you the phone, if you just accept a kiss from me."

I think of how nice it would be to talk to Sher. How nice it would be to have him kiss me again like he did downstairs.

"Fine," I mumble, staring straight ahead.

"Then lay back," he says, moving aside.

"Nope, that wasn't the deal," I tell him, but Oscar pulls me backward and jumps on top of me, pinning my arms to my sides with his knees.

"It's definitely the deal," he says, lowering his chest down until it almost touches mine. His hair brushes my cheek as he whispers in my ear, "You just didn't ask for the details, Hale. And you know what they say...the devil's in the details."

His lips run like a sigh along the base of my jaw, warm and soft. He stifles a groan against my mouth and his fingers slide into my hair. I struggle to get my arms free, but he's still got me pinned at the wrists with his knees.

"Oh no you don't," he whispers into my mouth. "You stay right where you are and let me kiss you, like you promised."

He nips my collarbone and an electric current flows down my spine. It feels so good; I close my eyes tight and let myself drift into his kiss. He places a kiss where his teeth were a moment before, the sting taken away by the soft, moist, warmth and I arc off the bed a little to meet his body as it presses against mine, stretching up to meet his mouth.

The pressure on my arms suddenly disappears and I blink open my eyes. Oscar is still hovering over me, his gaze digging into mine and his mouth curled into a grin.

"You've been kissed, Hale," he says. "You can have the phone."

"No," I whisper back, threading my fingers into the hair at the nape of his neck, drawing him back down to me. "More."

"I'd like that too," he says. "But we've got a nosey house guest downstairs, for one, and for two, I don't like to be rushed when I start kissing you. What I plan on doing with you is going to take time. Hours. Days, even. And since it's going to be all new to you, I want you to learn how to enjoy it."

I drop back onto the mattress with a puff. Oscar takes the phone from the nightstand and lays it beside me.

"All yours," he says. "Are you ready to be all mine?"

"Stop it."

"I'm serious," he says and,, since his expression reflects it as much as his tone, I just ignore him as I hold the phone over my head and dial Sher's number.

#

"Where the hell are you? Are you okay?" Sher blasts through the phone as soon as she hears my voice. I have to pull the phone away from my ear for a second.

"I'm fine. I'm at a beach house."

"With Ocker?"

"Yeah," I say as Sher inhales dramatically.

"Oh my God oh my God, oh my God! Did Ocker kidnap you? Wait. Did you dad just let him take you away? Your dad didn't even want you dating! Are you married? Oh my God, Hale, you're like one of those captive brides! Is this perv building a harem or something? Are you a Sister Wife? Oh my God, he's in a cult, isn't he? Wait. Are you still a virgin?"

"Slow down," I say the words slowly for emphasis, but my cheeks heat up. Oscar is reclined in the catcher's-mitt-chair, a finger on his temple and one on his jaw, watching me. I hope he can't hear Sher across the room, but when I hold the phone away from my ear, I can hear her loud and clear. I flip over onto my other side, putting my back to him.

"I'm just staying here for a while," I say.

"Staying or tied to a closet bar?"

"Staying. He invited me to his dad's beach house and we're here with his friends."

"What about the whole marriage thing?"

I drop my voice. "I don't know about that yet," I say, and then, I feel Oscar slide onto the bed beside me. He curls himself against my back and murmurs into my hair, "Ask your friend if she wants to meet us at town hall to be our witness."

His proximity makes me forget everything we were just talking about. On the other end of the phone, Sher says, "Was that him? Did he just say that?"

"Yes," I say. "Ignore him."

"He's got a totally sexy voice. Who'd expect that from an Ocker?"

"Did she just call me Ocker?" He chuckles near my ear.

"Oh my God, did he just hear me?" Sher squeals.

"Yup," Oscar says over my shoulder. He puts out a hand for the phone. "Let me talk to her."

"He wants to talk to *me*?" Sher's voice rises to chipmunk altitude. I shake my head, but Oscar grabs the phone from me and swings away to sit on the edge of the bed.

"Hello?" he says and his voice is all deep and caramel-y. I know Sher is probably peeing herself on the other end.

"Uh," I hear her giggle, "hi."

"So you're Hale's best friend?" he asks. He's met with more rapid-fire giggles.

"Mmm hmm."

"It's good to meet you then," he says. "I was wondering if you could tell me a little about Hale?"

I swoop over his shoulder and try to shout into the phone, "No, don't tell him anything, Sher!"

I doubt she can hear me through all the giggling. I doubt she's even breathing properly. She doesn't really answer, so Oscar just goes ahead and asks anyway.

"Can you tell me what her favorite food is?"

Sher bubbles, "Apples!"

"Interesting," Oscar says, turning to give me a raised eyebrow. "What are her hobbies?"

"She reads everything. All the time."

"She did mention reading," he says. Sher giggles even more. "What's her favorite color?"

"Purple!" she squeals.

"Purple," Oscar repeats. I make a grab for the phone, but he twists out of my reach. "Lavender or violet?"

"Violet!"

I groan and drop my hand over my eyes.

"You definitely know Hale," Oscar says. Sher finally stops giggling.

"Well yeah, she's my best friend," she says.

"Since you are, would you do us the honor, Sher..." he begins, but Sher shrieks into the phone, "YES!"

Oscar laughs. "Would you be a witness when we get married?"

"YES, YES, YES!" Sher shrieks again. I tear the phone out of Oscar's hand and he lets it go with a smirk.

"Hello!" I bark into the phone to calm Sher down.

"Oh my God, you're getting married! I'm going to be your bridesmaid! I can't believe it!" Sher's screaming. She's so excited that I want to just float along on the whole fairy tale with her.

"Nice, bestie," I mumble at her, trying to press down my smile. "Whose friend are you anyway?"

"Yours!" she squeals. "And his! I think I love him already!"

Oscar struts across the room. "My mission here is complete," he says, as he reaches the top of the stairs. He flashes me the peace sign. "Ocker, out."

His smile beams, satisfied, as he tromps down the stairs.

#

After whatever the kissing led to, between Amy and Landon, by the time I come downstairs, Amy is sitting primly at one end of the couch, as if she's being punished. She looks up when I step into the living room and frowns at me.

"Do you know where Oscar is?" I ask. Amy's gaze makes goose bumps jump up on my arms. She gives me her hard stare a moment before she shakes her head.

"Where did you come from?" she asks.

"Upstairs..."

"No, I mean, where did you meet him? Who are you?"

"Our fathers knew each other..."

"How long?"

"They grew up togeth..."

"I've known him for the last two years and he's never mentioned you," she says. Her eyes narrow. The guilt of what's happened to Sophia overwhelms me, as her best friend stares me down.

"I didn't mean for anything to happen between Oscar and me," I stammer.

"Hard to believe," Amy snaps. "Especially since you've got him wrapped around your pinky. He doesn't even seem to notice there's anyone else in the room besides you."

"It's not like that," I say, but I have to look away to lie, because I know how Oscar's eyes follow me. Amy doesn't buy any of it.

"It's exactly like that," she says. "He didn't even look at Sophia like that and he was so totally into her—but you—he's enchanted with you. It's like you're a witch or something."

It's not the kind of thing you say 'thank you' to. Amy's face remains pinched as she drills me with her eyes. We stay locked in our positions: she, staring bitterly from the couch, and me, frozen on the braided rug until I hear a car door slam. At first, I'm scared to pieces that Oscar might abandon me to go to the store with Landon that the two of them might leave me behind with this viper of a girl, but then something even worse happens.

The front door swings open.

"Ames! Where's OC? Aren't you guys making dinner yet? One of you could've given me a ride up here, you know!" Sophia says.

CHAPTER EIGHT

SOPHIA FOLLOWS AMY'S UNWAVERING GAZE to me, like a trail to dynamite. Her eyes travel up my legs slowly, pausing at my waist, again at my boobs, assessing my hair and, finally, resting on my face. I do the same to her. Sophia of the Pretty Names should also be Sophia of the Pretty Faces. I expected her to be pretty, but expecting is nothing like seeing her standing in front me.

"Who are you?" she asks.

"Hale," I say weakly. Sophia gives me a confused grin and looks back to Amy.

"Josh's girl?" she asks, but Amy shakes her head. Sophia turns to observe me again, with a curious, puppy-tilt of her head. "Who else did Oscar invite? Not Rosen?"

"No," Amy says. The sunroom door bangs, and we all turn to see Oscar and Landon.

"Hey, Soph," Oscar says. Sophia doesn't seem to hear the awkward casualness in his voice. She lights up with a warm smile for him. "Didn't expect to see you up here."

"Bet your ass you didn't," Amy grunts.

The excited light trickles out of Sophia.

"We were supposed to have Landon's birthday. I took off work," she reasons softly. Oscar's eyes flash to me, and Sophia catches it. She glances at me, then back to Oscar. "Who is she?"

"This is Hale," Oscar says. "And you and I need to have a talk, Soph. In private."

Landon crosses the room to the couch and taps Amy on the shoulder. "We should go into town and get that stuff we were talking about," he says. Amy shrugs him off, but she stands and grabs her purse off the corner of the inflato-bed.

"You want to come with us, Hale?" Landon asks. One sour glare from Amy reinforces how little I want that to happen.

"No thanks. I'm going to go upstairs and read," I say, even though I don't have any books with me. Sophia and Oscar remain like statues in the middle of the room as Amy and Landon go out the front door. I escape up the stairs, but Sophia's voice chases after me.

"Why is she going upstairs? Who is that girl, Oscar?" she asks. I sprint up the steps and fling myself onto the bed. I climb under the covers and hide from the impending conversation, the way I once hid from monsters in my closet.

"Let's go outside," I hear Oscar suggest.

"You want me out?" Sophia asks. There is a long pause, followed by their footsteps crossing the floor. I hear the gritty scrape of the sunroom door and the bang as it closes. I wait for the door to open again, for Sophia to charge through and hustle up the steps to me, but after several minutes, I creep out of the bed to the window. The overhang and trees obscure anything right below, but I twist the handle on the window and push it open. Their conversation washes in. I fold myself up on the floor to listen.

"I didn't expect it to happen like this," Oscar says, "but I'm relieved it did."

"Why do you keep saying that?"

"Come on, Soph. It's over. I know what you've been doing."

"Me? What am I doing? You're the one that snuck away and brought some girl up here. So what exactly am I doing to you?"

"You've been cheating on me, and I found out about it," Oscar says flatly. "The guy tracked me down to confront me."

"Who?" she shouts.

"I don't know his name. He didn't give me one."

"What did he look like? Because I have no idea what you're talking about!" she shouts at him. "You're the one that disappeared, and I had to find out from Amy that you were up here! And you've got a girl up here with you!"

The silence that follows makes my skin itch. I lean my ear closer to the window. Sophia's voice finally floats up, weak and watery.

"Oscar," she breaks down in hiccupping sobs, "Tell me what's going on. I don't get it. Someone's got to have me mixed up with someone else."

"The guy knew you by name, Sophia. He knew my car. He knew my name. He *told* me that you two had been seeing each other. He told me he'd been seeing you and he wanted me gone." Oscar says.

"Don't you know I would never do that?" Sophia whispers through her sniffles. "None of this is true. Why aren't you getting that? Some weirdo says something about me and you just automatically think it's true? Why wouldn't you even bother to ask me?"

More silence. It drags out so long, I lean my head on the window and the hinges squeak. I worry for several seconds that Oscar and Sophia heard it down below, but then they begin talking again.

"Maybe you're not lying" Oscar's voice sounds confused and distant.

"Of course I'm not," Sophia says. "You know I love you. I'd never cheat on you. I don't know who that guy was, but it's not true. It's not."

"I believe you," Oscar says. He sounds disturbed, and miserable, and relieved, all at once.

"Did you get with that girl because you thought I was cheating on you?"

"No," Oscar says, and then he tells her the lie he said he would. "I met her because our fathers are doing business together."

"Oh," Sophia squeaks the tiny word, and I hear her trying to choke back new sobs. "So where does this leave you and me?"

Oscar doesn't answer her question. Instead, he says, "If you don't know who that guy was, Sophia, than there's something even bigger going on. Somebody's trying to mess with me."

"Who?"

"I don't know, but I have an idea. Someone who was after more."

"Tell me."

"Not until I know for sure," he says. I wonder if he's looking up at the window. If he's talking about my dad. Or me.

I want to go home.

And then I hear Sophia say, "Oscar? I don't care what you did with that girl up there. I don't. I don't even care that you doubted me. I still love you, and I'm sorry this all happened."

"I'm sorry it happened too, Soph," he says softly.

I start to feel like I've got the flu. I wipe my palms on the edge of my shirt. I picture him down there, scooping her up in his arms and kissing her. That same kiss he gave me, pulling her lip through his teeth, sending Kryptonite into her legs.

I don't want to hear anymore. I crank the window shut as quietly as it will allow, get to my feet, and scoop up my bags. Oscar took his phone with him, or I'd call Sher. Or maybe just a taxi. Anyone that could get me out of here so that Oscar and Sophia can get back to being Oscar and Sophia without any Hale to get in the way.

I head for the stairs, but before I even get to the top, I hear his footsteps jogging up. Maybe he's going to take me home. Maybe he's coming to throw me out. I back away from the stairs, and when he hits the top step, Oscar catches the bags hanging off my shoulders, and his brow hikes upward in surprise. He closes the bedroom door behind him and clicks the lock.

"You going some place?" he asks.

"Yeah," I hang my head, worried to say the wrong thing. "I figured I'd just get out of here. Looks like you and Sophia have some stuff to work out."

Oscar's gaze flicks to the window that I had open a moment ago, then back to me. He takes a step toward me, hands up as if he's going to wrap them around my arms, but I shuffle backward. He drops his hands and his voice.

"What's going on, Hale?"

"Nothing. But your girlfriend's here now, and I don't want things to get any weirder than they already are."

"She's not my girlfriend anymore," he says. This time, he moves toward me and I move away, but he keeps coming, backing me up across the room.

"It's okay," I tell him. "You don't have to lie. I'm relieved. We don't have to go through with all of this now."

"You're relieved?" The sadness that arcs across his face and doesn't jar my sympathy at all. He's downstairs telling Sophia he's still in love with her, and now he's backing me into corners, acting like he's so sad that I want to leave. Sher was right. He wants a harem. It makes me want to punch him in the mouth.

"I'm leaving," I say. He's backed me into the middle of the room. I shift to one side, to walk around him, but Oscar shifts too, blocking my way. I move to the other side and he moves too. I drop my bag, pull back, and swing for his face.

Oscar catches my hand and, like lightening, he spins me around and pins my arm behind me, right between his chest and my back. I lift my foot and try to bring it down on his instep, but he jumps free, jerking me back with him. Wiggling in his grip, I try to slam my head backward into his nose and hit something that makes him curse, but he doesn't let go. He tightens his hold on me.

"Don't do that again," he growls in my ear through gritted teeth.

But I do. I try to swing back my head again, but he twirls me around. I stumble and hit the floor. It knocks the wind out of me, and he's on top of me before I can recover enough to kick him in the balls. He gets my hands in his and holds them, while I thrash uselessly beneath him.

After a few seconds, I realize I'm not going anywhere. My hair is stuck to my face, and I puff to get it out of my mouth. Still pinned, Oscar smiles down at me, as if we're just playing a game, except that a bruise is spreading across his cheekbone. I got him after all.

"You all done?" he asks. He's breathing harder than he wants me to know.

"Get off me," I say.

"Not until you calm down."

"I said get off me."

"What are you going to do about it?" he laughs.

"I was trying to do something about it," I tell him. "Get off and I'll go. You can play house with Sophia. She wants to."

"I don't care what she wants," he says.

"There's no reason for us to go through with any of this now," I say. "Sophia didn't cheat on you. This doesn't have anything to do with her."

"No, it doesn't," Oscar says. "But it doesn't change anything between us either. What's happened, happened, Hale. You need to quit fighting me on it."

"You're in love with someone else and you should be with her!" I grunt from under him.

"I'm not going to be with her. I'm marrying you," he growls. He exhales a warm and aggravated sigh against my neck, and then his lips are back at my ear. "I gave my word to that and, just so you know, I'm finding it incredibly easy to embrace the idea. Except when I have to pin you to the floor."

I take advantage of having his neck so close to my mouth and bite him. I sink my teeth just hard enough that he yelps and loses his grip, so I can wiggle away. He rolls onto his heels as I scuttle away from him. My back hits the edge of the bed. He lifts his hand to his neck, draws it back and checks for blood. I can see the red marks of my teeth on him, but no broken skin.

"Someday soon," he says with a patient laugh, "you're going to do that because you want me as close as you can get me, instead of further away."

The front door opens, and Amy's voice interrupts my response. "What the hell is going on? Why are you sitting here all alone?"

#

"I'll just go," Sophia says. Oscar dragged me downstairs by my hand to find Sophia sobbing at one end of the couch, and Amy bunched up beside her, shooting daggers at us as we enter the room.

"What's the matter with you?" Amy hisses, but she's looking at me instead of Oscar.

"I'm sorry, Sophia, but I think it's a good idea if you go too," Oscar says. "We'll talk another time, okay?"

"Sure," she says, rising off the couch. Landon, arms crossed on his chest and leaning on the front door frame, moves out of her way. Amy throws up her arms in frustration, and walks out after her friend. The door bangs shut.

"This isn't the birthday I was expecting," Landon jokes. Oscar runs a hand through his hair.

"Sorry buddy. I didn't expect it to go like this either."

"You want us to just take off?"

"No, no," Oscar says. "Stay. Your birthday's tomorrow. You're not driving home all night. Hell no."

"It's no big deal. Amy might be pissy all weekend anyway."

"We'll get her over it," Oscar says, but I can't imagine how it's going to happen unless I'm the one that goes home.

Sophia's tail lights finally glow like angry eyes through the front windows, as Amy lets herself back in. Landon gives her a win-some-lose-some grin, and she returns a scowl.

"How about we eat?" Landon suggests, trying to change the mood.

"You want to grill?" Oscar asks. They go off into the kitchen together and I trail them, so Amy doesn't jump me in the living room and eat my face. I think both guys know it's a real possibility too, since they don't try to assign us to salad chopping or side dish prep, while they escape out to the grill.

While Landon shapes the burgers into disks, Oscar opens a can of baked beans and dumps them in a saucepan on the stove. Amy stays right between the guys, leaning on the sink, and I hover opposite them, near the fridge. Landon makes small talk that only Oscar responds to.

Finally, Amy asks, "Did Sophia do that to your face, O?"

"Nope," he tells her, stirring the beans and smiling at her. "This is what happens when you miss a step going up the stairs."

"You should put ice on that. It looks awful, poor baby," she says. The guilt sinks into me like pushpins. Amy crosses the room to my side, opens a cupboard, and pulls out a plastic baggie. She hands it to me, along with the steak Oscar threw in there from our shopping trip.

"Better take care of your man, Hale," she says, but when she hands it all to me, she actually gives me a wispy smile. I'm totally shocked that she's not trying to use the steak to bludgeon me.

"That's right, Hale," Oscar jumps in, tipping his cheek in my direction, although he continues to stir the beans. "Take care of me."

If I didn't think that Amy would gut me for defying her, I would've lobbed the meat at Oscar's head and sent a bruise all the way to his hairline. Instead, I drop the steak into the plastic bag as I near Oscar, and lift the hard icepack to his face.

The bruise looks deep and sickly at the center, spreading out in purples and blues. Oscar hums, *mmmhhh*, when the cold touches his skin. His eyes close, the dark lashes resting momentarily on his cheek, and a nuclear blast of unintentional lust fires through me.

Oscar opens his eyes, and I realize how close I'm standing when he smiles. His eyes crinkle up first, and then, I notice his lips. He stops stirring and the beans bubble and blow steam.

"Kiss me," he murmurs, but suddenly I feel like the whole room is full of spotlights. I just smile and move back.

"The beans," I say. He frowns and pulls the saucepan off the burner.

"Burgers are ready to roll," Landon says and Amy says, "Thank God. I'm starving. Aren't you, Hale?"

I nod, but I'm completely confused. She wanted to pull my arms off a few hours ago, but she's smiling and talking to me now. I stick close to Oscar and he shoots me a conspiratorial grin, like he knows

I'm using him as a human shield against Amy. And he takes full advantage of it. He slips his arm around my waist, as we follow Landon and Amy out the sunroom door to the grill on the side of the house.

"I hear your dad and Oscar's work together, Hale. What does your dad do?" Landon asks as he lights the grill.

"They don't exactly," I begin, but Oscar cuts me off.

"Hale's dad likes working with his hands. He's starting up a premier environmental service and my dad thought his ideas were brilliant. You know how my dad is when he sees a good idea. He jumped in at the ground floor and plans to ride the elevator up. The company is already projected to go state-wide with the potential of multiple chains in less than two years."

I feel like my own mouth is hanging open. I thought Mr. Maree just bought my dad a truck and a tractor, not an environmental service dynasty.

"Wow, that's excellent," Landon, says.

"Yeah, it's really great," I say.

"So tell us about you, Haley." Amy says.

"It's just Hale," I tell her. She smiles dryly.

"Cool. Hale. Tell us about you."

"She reads more than anyone I know," Oscar says. "Her favorite color is purple, dark not light, she is picky about her Italian food, and she's an amazing cook. You should see what she can do with eggs."

"How long have you been together? I thought you just met each other?"

"We met about two weeks ago, but we just started dating this week," Oscar lies. "But it seems like I've known her for years."

"Cool," Amy says again with a tempered laugh.

"How about you two? How did you and Landon meet?"

"We met through Oscar and Sophia. Our best friends fixed up their best friends." Amy runs a hand down Landon's back. "But it looks like now it's going to be the four of us instead, so I guess I'm just gonna have to Girl-Up and make a new bestie."

"That'd be great," I say. Oh my God. Oscar presses his fingers into my side, and when I glance at him, he gives me a wink that says *Oh my God, don't let her be a bestie.* Or maybe I'm imagining it all.

As we eat dinner, Amy quizzes me on my life.

"Where did you go to school?"

"Lindbolm." I omit the fact that I just graduated a couple weeks ago.

"Lindbolm? I thought you were in college!" She laughs. "I was a Hyden girl. The guys at Lindbolm, though...oh my God. What do they put in your water over there? I swear all those guys had eight hands!"

"Are we really going to talk high school?" Landon says, reaching for another burger.

"You're right. I'm trapping us in Dullvania," Amy says, swooping in to drop a kiss that ends up only millimeters from hitting his eyeball. "Do you ever shop at Loot, Hale? I'm absolutely addicted to their lipstick line and their eye shadow palettes."

"Great. Make-up," Landon groans. "That's better."

"Loot's an awesome store," I agree. I don't mention that I've only been in the store a couple times and couldn't afford anything. I hope she doesn't suggest that we do a make-over, since all I've got in my collection are a couple drug store palettes with huge holes worn through the center of each color, an ancient tube of mascara, and a few eyeliner pencils that I have to warm up with a cigarette lighter.

Amy's cell rings and she turns to rifle through her purse, on the back of her chair, to get it. She holds it up and reads the screen with a frown.

"Poop. That was Soph," she says, shooting me an awkward grimace. "I better make sure she got home safe. Sorry. I'll take it outside."

"You don't have to do that," I say, but Amy's already scooted out the sunroom door. The three of us watch her shadow move toward the beach, her cell screen seeming to float away on its own, like a tiny, rectangular beacon.

"Anybody want coffee?" Oscar asks. But then his cell rings. He picks it up and peers at the screen. "I've got to get this. I'll be back in a sec."

He clicks on the phone and says, "Yeah, it's me, what's up?" before he goes out the front door. Landon and I are left at the table, me shooting glances toward the front door and him shooting them toward the back. I pick at my food, wondering if Sophia hung up with Amy and called Oscar. Or if it is Oscar's dad with more bad news. Then I perk up, imagining its Sher, calling to gush about a wedding plan, which sends an unexpected little tinge of enjoyment down into my stomach. Sher's enthusiasm about Oscar makes everything feel a little less scary, and like it will all turn out okay eventually.

Landon reaches for the bag of chips and peels his eyes from the shadows out the sunroom window long enough to ask, "So, you're good with jumping into the Maree clan?"

I blink at him a few seconds, not sure what Oscar's told him, what he knows. I finally settle on giving Landon a friendly smile and say, "Yeah, I'm good."

"He's a good guy," Landon says, looking into the bottom of the chip bag. "I know you two are moving fast, but you seem like a good person, so I hope it works out for you. Just wanted you to know that."

"Uh, thanks," I say, shifting around on my chair. I'm so uncomfortable; I'm actually starting to wish that Oscar would come back. But Amy comes in first.

"That was sad," Amy says, dropping her phone on the table. I don't know if she's talking to me or Landon. "Poor Soph. She wanted me to talk to her the whole way home."

"Long ride," Landon says, digging into the chip bag again.

"She'll be fine," Amy says, and this time, she shoots me a sympathetic glance. "Sorry to bum you out with all of this, hon. It's such a weird thing to be comforting one best friend and listening to her complain that her ex is a dickhead, when I've got a new friend sitting here who's in love with the same guy. Especially when I adore the guy, and he's friends with my boyfriend. It's just tough, you know?"

"It's okay," I mumble. I get it, but, when she said Oscar was a dickhead, the hair on my skin still bristled up.

Oscar walks back in a few minutes later.

"Everything okay?" Landon asks and Oscar nods.

"All good," he says. "You guys done eating? I was thinking of taking Hale for a walk down the beach."

"I want to go," Amy says, but Oscar gives Landon a wry smile and Landon reaches for Amy's hand.

"I think they want to be alone," he says, and then, with an eyebrow wiggle to her, "so *we* can be alone too."

"You are just the sexiest man I've ever met," Amy says, reaching over to squeeze Landon's cheeks. She does a hair flip to look at us, strands falling perfectly over one, seductively drooped eye. "Okay, you two, get out so I can be alone with my man."

Oscar pulls my chair back and takes my hand. We walk through the kitchen, stopping to retrieve a battery-powered lantern from a cupboard.

"Just leave the light on out front, so we can find our way back when you're—when you're good with us coming back in," Oscar says to Landon with a wink.

CHAPTER NINE

WHEN IT'S DARK OUTSIDE IN THE COUNTRY, it's black. Walking away from the house, there are no streetlights and no other houses around to light our way. The sound of the water on one side and the glow of the lantern on the sand in front of us is disorienting, and I still feel like I'm going to fall on my face.

"To get to the bigger beach, we've got to go down this path," Oscar says, taking my hand. I'm grateful for his touch and that he holds back the branches that would probably poke out my eyes otherwise, as we pick our way down the path. But a rustle in the tall grass along the side scares me even closer to him. I squeeze his hand, and his laugh rumbles.

"Nothing's gonna get you out here, Hale," he says. "Everything's way more afraid of you than the other way around."

But another rustle from the dark grass presses me to his side. I'm so close that his chuckle vibrates against me. The ground is uneven beneath my feet, and Oscar catches me a few times, hauling me up like a toddler, when I stumble. We go along for an agonizingly long time before we finally break through to the edge of long beach.

There is only a long strip of sand that rises up to a dark tree line on one side, or smoothes out to the black water on the other side. We plod along the beach until we're a ways away from the path. Oscar switches off the lantern.

"Want to sit and talk?" he says. Even when the lantern was on, there wasn't enough light to see further than five feet. I'd be lost in seconds. But with the lantern off, it's so dark that I can't even make out Oscar unless I'm staring off to one side of him.

"I guess." I sit, the sand surprisingly cold beneath me. Oscar drops down next to me, digging in his heels and resting his elbows on his bent knees. When my eyes get used to the dark, I can see his profile, but can't make out his features at all.

"Who called you?" I ask.

"That's what you've been thinking?"

"Yes. And that this sand is colder than I thought it'd be."

Oscar scoots a little closer and, I hate to admit it, but I'm grateful for the warmth of his body too. He leans back, propping an arm behind me and we're suddenly even closer, even though he's not really touching me at all.

"Are you going to tell me who called?" I ask.

"Of course," he says. "My father called first. He said there haven't been any new developments. He said all the news stations aren't re-broadcasting the story over and over—I guess Rick Tatum was just a regular guy, so it's not big news. The hardest part is going to be living with it. Even though the whole thing was kind of self-defense, and the guy dying was an accident, we've all got to live knowing that we are the only ones who know what happened."

He doesn't have to explain it to me. The dark cloud has been there for me too, ever since I found out what happened. Even without the marriage deal that our fathers made, knowing that the four of us are the only ones who know about a man's death leaves me with the dark feeling too. It's like I can get my mind off it, but there's still a smudge on every moment, a smoke ring that hovers around the edges.

"My father mentioned that your dad is kicking some ass with the new business. He's already got a few dozen clients, and he's been working non-stop."

"Good," I say. I don't want to think about my dad a whole lot. All I come back to is how he handed me over to Oscar that last night, kicking me out with my bags, and busting the bottles on the wall to make me leave. The bits of glass that cut me have become nothing more than tiny scars in my skin, another bit of smoke that I hope will eventually disappear. "Who else called?"

"Sophia," he sighs. "Amy probably got my number off Land's phone, and now Sophia's got it."

I don't want to talk around the edges of what's going on anymore. I cut right to it.

"Do you still love her, Oscar?"

He ducks his head down for a moment, between his elbows, and then he says, "Yeah, but not like you think."

"What do I think?"

"I'm guessing you mean do I love her, like *love* her. I don't. Not like that," he says. "But she was someone I cared about before, so I don't like to see her upset now. At the same time, I can't change the way I feel about you, just to suit her."

His phone rings in his pocket. He fishes it out and holds it up. It's Sophia. He flicks on the phone and says hello. Just like Sher, Sophia's a loud cell phone talker and I can hear every word.

"Oscar? What you're doing sucks. It really, really sucks. You go missing, and I have to track you down just to find out that you've been cheating on me? You should've respected me a little more and just handled this like an adult. I don't know where you get off giving me that bullshit story about *me* being the one who was cheating on *you*! And how long have you even been with that girl? You can't be in love with her! You can't!"

"Sophia," Oscar says calmly. "I'm sorry it happened like this with us. I didn't mean for it to happen, but..."

"Damn it!" she explodes. "Don't you dare tell me again how it's you and not me! It *is* me, or you'd be with *me* right now!"

"I wish I..."

"Don't keep saying you wish it didn't happen like this! It did happen!"

"I don't know what you want me to say, Sophia."

"I want you to say that you made a mistake!"

"But I didn't," Oscar says, "and I don't know what else I can say about it. I didn't mean to hurt you, but..."

"But you did."

"I suppose so," he says. "But I didn't mean to."

Sophia hangs up on him. Oscar touches the buttons that turn off the phone, before he slips it in his pocket.

"Sorry," he tells me. "I don't know what I can do for her."

"You broke her heart."

"That's what she tells me," he says, "but she doesn't believe that I didn't expect this to happen either."

"Did you tell her about Rick Tatum?"

"No, but I wasn't referring to that. I was talking about meeting you."

"Oh," I say. I'm glad it's dark out, glad that he can't read my expression or my blushing. I try to change the subject. "You haven't told anyone about what happened? Not even Landon?"

"No," he says. "But Landon does know that I plan to marry you. He knows our fathers are working together and that, the moment I met you, it was over with Sophia."

"What'd he say to that? That you're crazy, right?"

"Not at all. I think you're forgetting that Sophia and I were only together a few months. Land knew that things weren't perfect with us. When I told him about you, he told me to do what makes me happy. That's Land."

"He told me that at the kitchen table too, when you were outside on the phone with your dad."

"When Land says something, he means it."

"What about Amy? Does she mean it?" I ask. "She went from hating me to wanting to be my best friend. She's kind of scary."

"Not really," he says, as though he means to say she is. "I think of her as more determined than scary. When she gets something in her head, she's determined that that's the way it should be, but when she changes her mind, she changes it completely. Does that make sense?"

"Kind of," I say. "She still freaks me out though."

"Don't let her. You're with me and that's that. Amy will figure it out, if she hasn't already," he says. "What about you? Have you figured it out?"

"That I have to go through with this? Yeah, I figured that out," I say.

"That's all you've got?" The disappointment in his voice is darker than the shadow of his face. His head scoops down toward mine. "Hale, don't you have any feelings for me?"

Oh my God, what do I say? Do I tell him that he surprised me, and melted me, and that he's worn me down to the point of accepting the whole idea? Do I say that I'm falling in love with him, when I've never done it before and have no idea if that's really what this is? Do I tell him that the chemistry churning between us has made me want to wad up my virginity and throw it right at him? I have no idea what to say, so I play it safe and say, "I'm really starting to like you, Oscar."

"You *like* me?"

"I do."

"Oh Hale," he chuckles. "I want more than that from you. A lot more."

I see why Oscar wanted to take a walk on the beach now. He's got me in the eye of a perfect storm. His warmth prickles against my ribs, and the waves are lulling me with their methodic lapping on the shore. Most of all, the pitch darkness makes me feel like anything we say, or do, right now will be erased anyway, once we're back in the bright lights of civilization. Nothing matters except this moment. I feel brave beside Oscar's shadow and, when he leans closer to me, his breath dancing on my cheek, I don't move away.

"I want everything," he whispers. "Will you kiss me?"

In the darkness, my brave fingers reach for him, moving into the short hair at the nape of his neck. I pull him to me. I open my mouth against his lips and accept his tongue. His atomic waves come crashing through me all at once, and my entire body explodes in tingles. I let out a low moan that seems to get lost in his throat.

Oscar lays me back in the sand. He trails gentle kisses down my neck, pausing at my collarbone.

"Let me," he murmurs. I don't bother to answer or stop him as his hand slides beneath my shirt, his touch like a combination of radioactive particles that sends shocks of excitement blasting through me. I arch my back as he takes my breast in his palm, but this time, the moan we share is his.

His knee slides between mine. Oscar slips his arm beneath my back, while his mouth remains warm against mine. He lifts me off the sand, and pauses only long enough to peel away my shirt. The moment it is off, his reassuring, kiss returns.

The dark is so dark that it feels like my eyes are straining trying to see anything, so I just shut them and let my skin just feel. The sand is cold on my back and I shiver.

"Too cold?" Oscar asks. He sits up and pulls off his own shirt. He presses his bare skin to mine, and all my senses mix in delicious confusion. The definition of his muscular chest against my soft breasts, the heat of his skin on top of me, and the cold sand beneath my back, it all tangles into a beautiful kiss that engulfs my entire body. The begging words are suddenly in my throat, arching my spine again, but they dissolve as soon as his tongue warms my nipple.

I moan out loud again and Oscar stops long enough to murmur against my skin, "That feels good, doesn't it?"

I open my eyes as Oscar's lips move over my ribs. My ear is against the sand and in the darkness, a ways off, there is a sudden flash of light. It is a quick flash, but I see it, like a flashlight beam that grazes through the tree line and then dips out of sight.

"Oscar," I whisper, wiggling away while I try to cover the upper half of my exposed body.

"What's the matter?" He sits up, and I scoot around to cling to his back, raising my shadow-hand to point in the direction that I saw the light.

"I saw a flashlight." I whisper. We stare into the darkness. "Shine the lantern on it."

"The light won't reach. Are you sure it was a flashlight?" Oscar asks, when the light doesn't reappear. He waits a minute longer before turning to face me. "You know, it's okay, Hale. If we're moving too fast, you can just tell me, and I'll slow down."

"It's not—no, that's not what happened," I say, with a hot blush warming my face. "I saw a light, I swear I did."

"Maybe it was just a shooting star," Oscar says.

"On the ground?" I ask. "It wasn't a star, and there's nothing else out here."

"Exactly," he says. "I think you're just nervous. It's okay."

"I saw something," I tell him, swooping down to feel around for my shirt. I find it and slip it on, without shaking out the sand. Oscar retrieves his too, but doesn't put it on.

"Come on," he says, taking my hand. "Let's get back to the house."

#

Although we don't see a trace of any other flashlights, Oscar doesn't rub it in when we enter the wide ring of light cast by the beach house floods. We go in the front door, after Oscar announces us through the screen. Amy yells, *Come on in,* like her life's been ruined. She's sitting at the kitchen table, when we walk in.

"Landon's sick," Amy says, pointing to the bathroom. "Diah-screama. He's been locked in there, howling and hanging onto the towel rack, ever since you guys left."

"Serious?" Oscar says, and shouts toward the bathroom, "Land? You okay, buddy?"

"I'm going Sea Cucumber in here, baby," Landon hollers back. The toilet flushes. "Stay out!"

"No problem," Oscar says. "Hale and I can just hang out upstairs."

I gulp. Just like I suspected, back here under the regular lights, I feel a little more self-conscious and reserved. How good it felt to let go with Oscar, out on the beach, seems a little fast and loose now that Sophia's best friend is staring at me again.

"Hey, don't go," Amy says, before Oscar can grab my hand and drag me upstairs. "Let's play Scrabble or something. I don't have anything to do if Landon's locked in there all night."

"Sure," I say, but Oscar flashes me a look that is pure disappointment. I slide into a chair at the table and turn to Amy. "Were you out looking for us?"

"Outside?" Amy asks. "No, why?"

"I swore I saw a flashlight out there. This isn't hunting season, is it?"

"It's always some kind of hunting season," Amy says. "Good thing you didn't get your heads blown off."

Oscar, who had wandered out of the room, wanders back in with the Scrabble box. He lays it on the table and takes off the top.

"I think her eyes were playing tricks on her," he says, shooting me a grin.

"Out there?" Amy says. "There's no light to play tricks with."

"Thanks for helping," Oscar says. He lays out the board and tiles, as the toilet flushes again.

"Sophia's been blowing up my phone," Amy says. "She's saying you won't talk to her?"

"I tried," Oscar says. "Help me out, would you? Talk to her. I understand she's upset, but like you said, just a couple of weeks ago, she was thinking of breaking it off too. I wouldn't mind talking to her, if she'd listen to what I have to say."

"Oh no, she doesn't want to hear any of that," Amy says. She glances at me. "Don't worry about it. She's just slammed that you ended everything first, and had someone waiting in the wings. The rejection stings a little, but I'll straighten her out."

"I'd appreciate it," Oscar says.

We play two rounds of Scrabble, in which I seem to get the tiles that spell nothing more complicated than 'cat' and 'sit', but Oscar strings together 'x' words like *infix* and *Xis* that I challenge and lose on. Amy tries to make every word have some dirty root to it, spelling out suck, nip and lick, and then insists she should get extra points for working all her words into close proximity on the board. Landon flushes the toilet enough times that we lose count.

"Tomorrow," Amy says, when I object to another game. "Let's go shopping. There's that great outdoor mall..."

"What do you want there?" Oscar says.

"Stuff," Amy says, as if she can't believe he's asking.

"Oh...stuff. Actually, I could do with some stuff," Oscar laughs as the toilet flushes again. "If your old man can get off the toilet, we could."

"He'll be fine, I gave him a bottle of Pepto." Amy says. She leans back off her chair and shouts toward the bathroom door, "You're drinking the Pepto, right?"

"Yeah," Landon answers.

"Romantic weekend, his ass," Amy says, giving me a wink, and blowing some hair off her forehead. She smiles at me. "Better stack your wallet for tomorrow, Hale. We're going to be gone a while, because my man owes me all kinds of stuff tomorrow."

The bathroom door opens and Landon steps out, looking a little pale. "Stuff?" he says, closing the door behind him. "We're going on a stuff trip?"

"Yup, shopping. Our favorite," Oscar says with a dry smile. "You gonna make it there, buddy?"

"Hope so. Must've been the fish and chips I had in town."

"Poor baby," Amy croons, jutting out her bottom lip. "A shopping trip will make it all better."

"Sure will." Landon grimaces as Oscar grabs my hand and pulls me up out of the chair.

"We're going to hit the hay," Oscar says. I would object simply on the grounds that I don't want to be told what I'm going to do, but it's not like I've got options. There's no TV, no bookcases, no nothing, but Amy putting away the Scrabble board, and Landon fanning at the bathroom door with his newspaper. The prospect of staying down here, versus going up and fending off Oscar if I need to seems like a no-brainer.

We say our goodnights and skitter past the bathroom and up the stairs. I go in first, and Oscar closes the door behind me. I hear the snick of the lock and turn back to him.

"Just so you won't feel uncomfortable," he says, and his expectation sends a shot of resentment straight through me.

"You're making a pretty enormous assumption," I say, crossing my arms over my chest. "Just because things got nuts at the beach doesn't mean I'm just falling into bed with you now."

"It doesn't?" He tips his head to the side with a grin. He steps forward, and I step back. "You're shy now?"

"I lost my head," I say. His hands reach out and wrap around my waist.

"I could try and help you lose it again," he says, but he doesn't try to kiss me. He keeps his gaze on mine. I can't help it when my eyes dart away. Oscar brushes his thumb against my shirt to bring me back.

"Listen," he says. "I told you before, if it's going too fast, you just say so. We've got the rest of our lives to figure this part out. I don't need you to rush into it. What I need is for you to trust me."

"We're going too fast," I blurt. "I mean, I liked being on the beach with you, but--I just think—I don't know."

"Ok, I think I understand what you're saying," he says. "We'll just keep it at the beach level for a while, okay?"

"Okay," I say, but even agreeing to 'beach level' feels kind of dirty. Then again, when I think of his hands on me, an excited shiver radiates over my skin, covering me in goose bumps. I'm not going to say I don't want what happened on the beach to happen again, but I'm not sure that it's going to feel like that again either.

I stand there, rigid, waiting for him to try to kiss me or make a move for the edge of my shirt. But he doesn't. Instead, Oscar reaches into his pocket, takes out his phone, and steps away, touching buttons to turn it back on.

"If you want to talk to your friend, after I check my messages..." he begins, holding the phone to his ear. He frowns, presses his finger to the screen, listens, and frowns again. I scoot closer to listen. My stomach turns upside down, as he repeats the action several times. He paces across the room, too far for me to hear anything but a nondescript murmur that is probably actual yelling up close. He turns the phone off and hands it to me.

"What's the matter?" I ask, taking it from him.

"Sophia," he sighs, turning away to remove his shirt. He draws the fabric over his head, and I almost forget what he said the moment the weave of his back muscles are exposed. I suck in a breath and bite my lip, so the pain will jar Sophia's name loose.

"What did she say?" I ask. His skin is such a perfect shade of brown, as if he's been poured from a cappuccino machine. I think of how Sher once said she had fantasies about covering a boy she liked in whip cream. I lick my lips at the thought of sliding my tongue over Oscar's sweet, cappuccino skin.

"I don't know. I'm not listening to the messages. She's taking this way too hard."

"What do you mean?"

"The first message, she said we needed to talk, but she sounded pretty calm. Then she left a message that just said *call me*. Then, *Call Me NOW*. The last one, she was yelling. Hale, we were together for three months. Not years, months. We tried making it work, but it's not like we were the perfect couple. We were having problems from the start."

"Like what?"

"She was always going out with her friends. I didn't mind a few girls' nights, but even our time together was always a group event. I got tired of it never being just the two of us. Then, I found out that all the girls' nights were always at a nightclub. The main reason I have for going to a nightclub is to find a girl. She didn't see it as a problem if she danced with other men, as long as she ended up at my house at the end of the night. But I had a big problem with it."

Faithful, loyal. That's the problem that he means. I'm beginning to feel like I know him better than Sophia ever did.

"Didn't you ask her not to go?"

"Sure," he says. "She insisted she was never doing anything, but I thought it was disrespectful that she went at all."

"That's why the thing with Rick Tatum..."

"It made perfect sense," Oscar finishes for me, "but when she came up here, and I spoke to her, she didn't seem to have a clue as to what I was talking about. I don't know that she could've faked it that well. All her calling seems a little psycho, but Sophia isn't nuts. I think she was as shocked to find out about you, as I was to hear about Tatum, but now I really don't think she had a clue who he was."

"Then who sent the guy?" I ask.

My stomach turns to lead. I'm scared to death that he's going to say he suspects my father. Ever since I overheard him wondering to Sophia, I've wondered too, if my father could be capable of doing something so devious, just to get some money out of an old friend. It seems impossible, but so does the idea that my father would make a deal and just hand me over like livestock, to marry his friend's son. The part that still confuses me is how my father could just accept it all; how easily he accepted the truck and the tractor service, how easy it was to give me away to marry a stranger.

And, if Oscar suspects my father, he will suspect me too. I don't know what that will mean, if I am married to him. I don't know what it will mean, if I've fallen in love with him. I am hardly breathing when Oscar says, "I don't know yet. But don't worry. I'm going to find out."

"Do you think it's anyone you know?"

"Yes, I think it might be," he says, turning his sharp gaze to me. "But I'm not going to falsely accuse anyone, Hale, so that's all I'm saying for now."

"Okay," I squeak. When he's stripped down to his boxers, it's not like I don't notice every inch of him, but I'm just too worried now. What if it was my father? I want to ask, to know if that's what he's thinking, but I'm scared of what the answer might be.

Oscar slips under the sheet, folding his arms under his head. He's watching me now, the sharpness in his gaze replaced by an almost sensual look of observation. I'm still standing in the middle of the room, just standing there, like a dumb ass.

"You going to call your friend?" he asks.

"Uh, yeah," I say, and turn my back to him, as I walk to the mitt-shaped chair. I fall into it, curl up my legs, and dial Sher. She picks up on the second ring.

"You have to call me MORE THAN ONCE A DAY!" she hollers. She's not upset though. She's just being Sher. I laugh.

"Sorry," I tell her. "I'll try."

"So what have you been doing?" she asks. I really can't tell her everything I want to, not with Oscar watching me. But, typical Sher, she doesn't give me much time to answer. "What's going on with Oscar? DON'T TELL ME YOU'VE HAD AN OSCAR MEYER YET? OH MY GOD!! I'm going to be the last virg on EARTH!"

I twist in the chair, so I can put as much of my back to him as possible, and whisper into the phone, "No. Shut up, okay? That didn't happen."

"But it's going to!" Sher squeals.

"Stop. Seriously," I say. Sher lets out a long *oooooooh*.

"Oh man—he's there right now, isn't he?" she whispers back.

"Mmm hmm."

"Just say yes or no, then. Have you *tasted* the Oscar Meyer yet?"

"Ugh," I hide my eyes beneath one hand. "No!"

"Alright, alright. Have you even seen it?"

I chew on my thumbnail. "No."

"Has he seen your poof?"

"No!"

"Don't be touchy. He's had you a few days, and I need to know if you're going to come back damaged."

"Stop. Again."

"Well, you know you are. You can't go get married and not break your hymen."

"I will hang up this phone right now if you don't stop talking."

"Fine. Okay. So, has he squeezed the melon? Felt around the first floor? Nuggled with a hobbit?"

I laugh at that one. "What did you just say?"

"You know what I mean. Did he?" she asks. I chew my thumbnail again.

"Yes."

"Oh my GOD!" she shrieks and I have to pull the phone away from my ear so she doesn't shatter my eardrum. Oscar chuckles from the bed, and I try to fan my hair over that side of my face to hide the blush.

"Last chance to shut up," I tell her.

"Was he good at it? Can he kiss, or is he all..." she makes noises in the phone that sound like she's been coated in peanut butter and is being mulled by a basset hound.

"Yeah, it's what you said."

"Good? Did I say good, or do you mean bad?"

"No," I blush, even with my face pointed toward the wall. "Good."

"YAY!" Sher hoots.

"Okay, I've got to go," I tell her. I want to keep talking, but I can't keep doing it with Oscar behind me. Not when he might be able to hear every fool thing that comes out of Sher's mouth.

"No! I miss you," she shrieks. "Don't go. There's nothing to do, and nobody to talk to anymore!"

"I miss you something horrible too," I tell her. "But I won't be gone forever."

"When will you be back?"

I realize I have no idea. "Soon," I lie. "We've got to go dress shopping, right?"

"I've been ripping out magazine photos for ideas. What color do you want to go with for the bridesmaid dresses?"

"I don't know. Whatever you want, I guess. You're the only one."

"I get to pick? But it's a big decision, Hale! It's huge!"

"And I want you to pick," I say.

"Ok, ok, ok," Sher says. I bet she's waving her hands in a panic. "Purple. It's your favorite color. Let's do purple."

"Whatever you want, Sher. You'd look really nice in red. You sure you don't want red?"

"That's whorey. You can't do whorey for a wedding."

"This one you could," I laugh, and she laughs too, but I can hear how she doesn't want to.

"Purple," she says. "I want purple, okay? It'll be gorgeous."

"Whatever you want is fine with me."

"I want you to be happy...and looking at a purple-covered bridesmaid. I've been babysitting Mrs. Carlson's kids to put some money away for it."

"Cool," I say. "We can go to Salvation Army when I get back."

"The thrift shop?" Oscar shouts from the bed. "You two aren't going to the thrift store for dresses. Tell Sher that I'm paying. Tell her not to worry about it."

"Oh my God, was that Oscar?" she says.

"Yeah," I tell her. "He says he wants to pay."

"He's so awesome, Hale. I think he really is."

"Maybe," I whisper into the phone with a tiny grin. I wind some hair around my finger. "Maybe."

CHAPTER TEN

I SLEEP ON TOP OF THE covers to prove a point. But when I wake up, I'm under the covers, sweating, with Oscar's heavy arm slung over my waist. As I try to slide away, he tightens his grip and pulls me against him.

"Don't go," he mumbles into my hair.

"We've got to get up. What time is it anyway? Amy's probably waiting to go shopping."

"If Landon's butt is cooperating," Oscar says. I wiggle out from under his arm.

"We won't know if it is, until we go down there," I say. Oscar rolls onto his back, watching, as I grab my bag. I pull out fresh clothes and my shoddy make-up case.

"What did you want to get today?" he asks. I shrug. I don't have any money, so I guess I don't really want anything.

"Nothing," I say, like it doesn't matter.

"I've never known a girl to go shopping and come back with nothing."

"Oh? How many girls have you shopped with?" I ask, trying to derail him from the fact that I don't have a penny to my name.

"A few," he says, his voice thoughtful, as I sweep up my hair and tie it in a messy ponytail.

"I'm going to go grab a shower. I'll be back," I say, as I escape downstairs before he can ask me anything else.

#

Landon, pounding on the door, cuts my shower short. I turn off the water and pull back the curtain, just in time to hear Landon's panicked voice begging me to get out of the bathroom quick. I wrap myself in a towel, grab my clothes, and squeeze past Landon, as he bustles into the bathroom, mumbling apologies before slamming the door shut.

"He was doing so good," Amy says. "He still thinks he wants to go, but we should probably wait until he comes out for our final answer, okay?"

"Sure," I say. I don't want to have a conversation with Amy, while I'm making a puddle on the floor, so I scramble up the stairs, but once I'm at the top, I realize I'm in an even worse position now. Oscar is dressed, and fastening his watch, as I walk in.

"You're wet," he says.

"Don't try to impress me with your genius abilities," I joke. He smiles, but he doesn't leave the room, so I say, "Landon might need somebody to roll the bottle of Pepto under the door. He's in the bathroom again. Don't you want to go downstairs now, and take care of your friend?"

"Want to? No," he says, taking a seat on the mitt-chair. He drops his voice to a whisper. "Especially when there's a wet woman in my bedroom and, even less so, if I have to be down there with Amy, all by myself."

"She's not the big bad wolf,"

"You don't know her very well," he laughs. "Besides, I don't want to miss what's happening up here."

"I'm not changing in front of you," I say. He lifts a brow quizzically. A challenge.

"I'm not," I repeat. I look away, out the bedroom window, so his gaze won't make me coward-out on what I want to say. "You told me that if I wanted to slow down, we could. You said that you wouldn't push me, but you are. What you're doing right now is pushing me."

Oscar gets to his feet.

"I guess you're right," he says. "Absolutely right. But I was hoping you'd trust me. I was hoping you'd want me to see you."

"I don't," I say.

"Okay," he replies. "I said I could wait, and I meant it. I'll be downstairs with the big bad wolf."

As he starts down the steps, I dress quickly, worrying that he might change his mind and come back up the stairs. And worrying about the part of me that wants him to.

#

"You're a warrior, buddy," Oscar tells Landon. "Just don't shit in my car."

"Very funny," Landon says. "It was better this morning. I drank another bottle of the pink stuff, so I should be good to go."

"Great," Oscar says, as we pile into the car. We drive for an hour, stopping twice, once at a gas station and once at a creepy diner, so Landon doesn't explode. Each time, Oscar tries to convince Landon to go back, but Landon insists we soldier on to the mall.

When we get there, Landon disappears for fifteen minutes while we stand at the entrance of the huge outdoor mall. We stand at the very tip of the cobblestone walkway, with shops stretching along either side, and with statues and trees rooted on manicured patches of grass in the middle. The cobblestones meander off to more shops to the left and right, and Amy's already gushing that the mall seems like it's a mile long. I can't imagine what kind of hell this must look like to Landon today.

He joins us again, a few minutes later, and says, "How about we go find some more Pepto while the girls go shop?"

"It's a plan," Oscar says. Amy kisses Landon, and Oscar wraps his arms around me in a tight hug. There's a tug on my pocket and I try to twist away, but Oscar doesn't let go.

"There's some money in your pocket for shopping," he whispers in my ear. "Have fun with it."

I don't wait. I reach into my front pocket and feel the wad of bills right away. I know what money feels like, and I can tell there's more in my pocket now than I've ever laid hands on in my entire life.

"I can't take this," I say. Out of embarrassment, I don't pull it out of my pocket. Amy is still making out with Landon, but if I were to pull a bank vault out of my shorts, I'm sure it'd draw attention.

"Of course you can," Oscar says. "You should have nice things, Hale. I want you to. Think of it as part of the deal."

"The deal." I frown and he catches it.

"I didn't mean it like that," he says. "Come on. Have fun with me. Go shopping and get what you want. Money is supposed to be enjoyed. Go enjoy some. That's all I meant."

"Okay," I tell him, even though I've never had that thought about money. Money is meant to be scrimped and pinched and wanted, but rarely has there ever been enough in my life to actually enjoy it. My fingertips feel along the smooth roll again. No matter what I plan to do with it, I'm not going to make a scene about it here, so I just say, "Thanks."

"You're welcome," he says, as Landon breaks away from Amy and motions to Oscar.

"Come on, OC. We need to embark on the Pepto hunt."

"We'll see you back here in two hours for lunch?" Oscar asks me.

"Yeah, yeah, yeah," Amy jumps in. "Two hours. Like that's enough time to even look at anything."

"Three hours, then," Oscar says. "Late lunch."

"Pepto!" Landon complains, and Amy agrees to three hours, dragging me away by the arm.

"Come on," she says. "We're going to have to do some serious power shopping to get done in three hours!"

#

Spending his money should be easier, but every time I think of reaching into my pocket, I just can't do it. I make excuses to Amy about colors not being right or not liking the styles, even though the truth is: I like all of it. Unlike the Salvation Army, when something catches my eye, there is a whole rack of them in my size.

"We *have* to go into Jake," Amy says, pulling me through the fancy doors of a dark store that has the deep smell of a man's cologne. Inside, the store isn't just racks of clothes. It has huge potted plants and sturdy shelves that make the place feel more like a hidden bungalow than a clothing store. The boy's clothing is mixed in with the girl's, so there are ascending hooks of boy's board shorts displayed beside a female mannequin dressed in an eyelet skirt and tank.

"That's gorgeous," she says, searching for one of the eyelet skirts in her size. "And I think Land should come back here and get a pair of those board shorts."

The idea lights up in my head. One of the salesgirls walks by, and I stop her to ask, "Can you tell me what kind of cologne I'm smelling? I could smell it when I first came in."

"Oh, let me see what we have in the scent burner," she says, and I follow her as she weaves our way to the register counter. She chatters at me over one shoulder while we go. "We have so many different scents, I think this one is called Force, but let me make sure."

She ducks behind the counter and then reappears, nodding. She points to one of the bottles lined up in a display on the counter.

"Yep, it's Force. This one. Would you like a bottle?"

"How much is it?"

"This size is only eighty nine dollars," she says. Only eighty-nine. In my world, one bottle of cologne equals about two weeks of groceries or almost a quarter of the rent. One of my lungs might've just fallen out of my mouth.

"I'm going to think about it," I say, as casually as I can.

"No problem," she says. "Just let me know if you'd like it, and I'll ring you up when you're ready."

At least she wasn't one of those mean types that raked her eyes over my frayed shorts and faded shirt with a smug smile. She just grins at me and then flits away to help a guy who can't find his size on the rack.

I bury myself in the aisles, back by the socks where no one seems to come. I figure I better know what Oscar gave me, in case I do want to buy something. I pull the roll of bills from my pocket, and almost pass out as I unroll the cash. It's all hundred-dollar bills; ten of them, all rolled up like a stubby, green cigar.

Holy shit.

It comes back to me; all of my dad's talk about the Maree's and their money, but it wasn't so real until this second. I know they gave my dad a truck and lawn equipment, I know Oscar has a nice car, but the beach house isn't over the top, and Oscar doesn't act like he's sitting on Fort Knox. He talks to me like we're equals. Although, looking down at the pile of cash in my hand, it's obvious that in some ways, we're nowhere near equal.

"Hey," Amy calls to me, looking over a shelving unit stacked stylishly with purses. "You're buying socks? Are you kidding me?"

"No," I tell her, stuffing the money back into my pocket. "I was just thinking of getting Oscar a bottle of cologne."

"Good little girlfriend," she beams. "I should probably get Land something too."

At the register, I pay for the bottle of Force, and Amy gets the eyelet skirt, a pair of sunglasses, a red string bikini, and a bottle of the same cologne for Landon.

"Now we won't know whose man is who's in the dark," she giggles, and I laugh, but I hope I don't run into Landon that way. She glances down at my small bag with the cologne in it. "You've got to get more than that! Come on, Haley, I'm going to make a shopper out of you, if it kills me!"

Amy doesn't shop for herself after that. Her entire focus is on me. She drags me into another clothing store, where I break down and buy a full-length nightgown. I had planned to spend Oscar's money on gifts for him, but Amy keeps insisting I need to buy something for myself. I pass by all the lacy, satin gowns until I find the one I want.

"You're classy, not slutty," Amy applauds me, eyeing the gown. It's got spaghetti straps, and it's made from lime green cotton, although there is some shiny lace work over the chest. Even so, the gown is one that I could've worn in front of my father without blinking an eye.

"Totally not slutty," I tell her, giving the cashier another hundred-dollar bill.

"Oscar really bank rolled the trip, huh?" Amy asks, motioning to the bill. "That was nice of him."

"I guess," I say. "It's kind of embarrassing, actually."

"Really? How come?"

It's a fair question, considering I led her right into it with my previous admission, but it is too complicated to answer without explaining everything, and I really don't know Amy that well. But I'm starting to feel a connection to her. Maybe it's just because she's stopped blaming me for Sophia, or because she seems so comfortable with me. I'm really starting to like how quick she is with her comebacks, and all the attention she's giving me. Most of all, it feels nice to have another girl to talk to, in Sher's absence.

"I forgot to bring any cash with me when we came up," I answer. I feel a little guilty for not telling her the whole truth, but Amy just nods.

"Good story," she giggles. "I'm going to have to remember that one for next time we come!"

I steer Amy away from Loot and into a men's shop across the cobblestone sidewalk. I buy Oscar two pairs of plaid pajama bottoms, in hopes that he'll keep them on at night, but no shirts. On the way to the register, I add a bunch of the little stuff I find on display: a money clip, a silk tie with a weird design that Amy assures me is totally *boss*, and a ridiculously fancy flashlight with an LED bulb that should shine further than the lantern we took to the beach.

Amy curses under her breath as she checks her phone. "It's time to go meet them," she says. "And we didn't even get to check out Loot yet."

She's so disappointed that I feel guilty for having dragged her into the men's store. I grab her arm and pull her in the direction of the make-up store.

"Come on, we can be a little late. We're girls, right?" I say, and Amy laughs as we walk through the front doors.

#

We're ten minutes late when we get out of Loot, and Amy's phone rings. She fishes it out of her purse and puts it to her ear.

"Hello?" she says sweetly. The volume is down so low, I don't know who it is, until she says, "Hi OC. Relax, we're coming. We just had to make an emergency stop at Loot, since Haley took so long buying you presents."

I want to kick her. It was supposed to be a surprise.

"Alright, already. We're coming!" she ends sullenly, clicking off the call. It rings before she has a chance to drop it in her purse. She frowns and puts the phone back to her ear.

"What now?" she asks. "Oh, get me a diet and the taco salad, no tortilla bowl. Yeah, just the salad, you know, leaves in a regular bowl? Get one for Haley too. She'll love it. Okay, bye."

"We're having Mexican?" I say.

"Hope you don't mind me ordering for you, but this salad is the best in the world. You'll thank me, I swear."

"Sounds good," I tell her, because I don't care what I'm going to eat. I'm more excited about giving Oscar his presents.

The restaurant is a longer walk than I expected. When we get there, Oscar pulls out a chair for me and I get tangled with the waiter who is trying to drop off our food.

"Would you step back, please, and let the lady sit down?" Oscar asks. The waiter, affronted, gives a stiff nod, but when Oscar stands, the waiter's eyes shift submissively to his feet. Oscar's body is powerful, and I hadn't really noticed it before, but when he throws his shoulders back, he's intimidating too. Once I'm seated, Oscar leans toward me and says, "I gave you the money to enjoy yourself."

"I did," I tell him. I don't go any further, and Oscar sits back with a smile, but doesn't ask me anything else. His phone rings, and he pulls it out of his pocket.

"Is it her again?" Landon asks, but Oscar shakes his head as he stands up and walks away from the table, with his phone to one ear and his finger blocking the other.

"Her who?" Amy says, picking up her fork and stabbing it into the tortilla-bowled salad. "Remember, I said no tortilla?"

"I told them," Landon says with a shrug. "And who do you think it is? Sophia's been blowing up his phone for the last hour. Hasn't she called you?"

"Yeah," Amy says, pushing a fork full of taco salad into her mouth. "She's just sad. I think he's doing the right thing by just letting her walk it off. I don't know why she's taking it this hard. Whenever I got turned down, I just went to the bar and picked another guy." Amy smiles at Landon. "How do you think I got you?"

"I think it just happened so quickly, it was crazy for both of us," I say. I really have no right to say anything, to interject myself into this circle of friends that predates my four-day relationship to Oscar.

"It did happen pretty much overnight, didn't it?" Amy agrees, and I'm instantly sorry I opened my mouth. Even though Amy's words are more curious than vicious, her gaze makes me squirm as she asks, "How do you think anyone can fall in love that fast?"

Oscar comes back, and lays his phone done by his plate as he takes his seat. He puts a cloth napkin across his lap and says, "What did I miss?"

"Not a thing," Landon says. I notice he's only got water in front of him, with a lemon wedge floating in it.

"Not eating yet?" I ask in order to change the subject.

"We ordered a bread basket," he says, rubbing his gut. "That should do it for me."

"Did you talk to Soph?" Amy asks Oscar. She pokes around her salad instead of looking at him, like it's no big deal.

"No, just business. Dull stuff," he says.

"Have you talked to her at all?"

"No," his voice is a little more stern. "And I don't plan to."

"Just saying, it's probably for the best at this point."

"I think so." Oscar says. He jabs his fork toward my salad. "Any good?"

"It's fine," I tell him. It's a salad. But when he smiles, I smile back, and the salad ends up being exactly what Amy said it was—the best in the world.

CHAPTER ELEVEN

OSCAR FLOPS ACROSS OUR BED. He's followed me upstairs, when I said I was going to put away the stuff I bought. I was planning on hiding one present under his pillow, but with him laying on it, hiding anything is kind of impossible.

"So," he says. "Amy said you bought me presents?"

"I did. But you can't have all of them right now."

"No?" his voice is a husky caress.

"Nope. You have to earn them."

"Alright, I'll play," he says. His eyes flash, and my stomach is shot straight through with a tingle that feels like melting ice crystals. "This sounds like it could be exciting."

I hadn't really thought about him earning anything, but the thought popped into my head, and it sounded exciting to me when I said it too.

"I'll let you know," I say. "But you can have one thing now."

I pick through the bags and find the first one. I hand it to him, and Oscar slips the boxed cologne out of the bag. He smiles, watching me, as he lifts the edge of the box to his nose.

"You like this..." he says and I nod. " I meant for you to buy things for yourself, not for me, Hale."

"I did buy something for myself."

"Show me," he says. He opens the box, removes the cologne, and puts some on, as I find the bag I want. I slide the nightgown from the bag and hold it up.

"It's pretty isn't it?" I say.

"It is. But I'd rather you wear nothing to bed."

A blush creeps up from my neck. "Don't say things like that."

"Why?" he says. "It's true."

"Because it makes me feel embarrassed."

He bites his lip.

"Ok, then I won't say it anymore," he says. "I'm sorry. I didn't mean for you to be embarrassed. I meant to let you know what I feel like whenever I lay down beside you."

"That was—embarrassingly sweet," I say. I pick up the bag with the tie and hand it to him.

"I earned one already?" He laughs. "This is going to be easy."

He reaches in, and pulls the tie from the bag. In the evening light, filtering in from the windows, it takes me a minute to recognize which present I gave him. It's not the tie that I picked out at the store. The clerk must've switched it by accident. The tie Oscar's holding is a funky olive green with cream, tie-dyed splatters. Oscar tries to smile as he stumbles for something nice to say. He holds it up and squints at it.

"It's, um..." He rubs it between his fingers. "It's nice?"

I break out in giggles, sitting down on the edge of the bed.

"It's hideous!" I squeal.

"I didn't want to say that."

"It is! That's not the tie I bought you! I got you one with a really cool design on it! Somebody mixed it up."

"Oh good," he says. "I was afraid I'd have to wear it."

"No, no," I laugh. "I wouldn't let you if you tried!"

Oscar steps closer to me. "Thank you," he says. "For the present."

"It's a present-fail," I giggle.

"You could always give me another," he says, but his eyes rove to the nightgown, and the hard blush creeps into my cheeks again. He lifts his hand to my face, cupping my cheek and rubbing his thumb on my skin. His tone drops into that lovely, deep thrum as he says, "I have something for you too."

"What?" I say and Oscar lifts the tie to eye level.

"Let me," he whispers as he places the soft tie over my eyes. My body goes stiff as he knots the tie at the back of my head. I can't see, but I'm aware of Oscar's heat leaving me. I hear his footsteps crossing the floor, the snick of the lock on the bedroom door, and his return gait.

"Are you okay?" he asks.

"I'm nervous. What are you going to do?"

"Just relax and let me," he says. His heat dances at my cheek and trails lazily down my jaw. His tongue moves over my mouth, and I part my lips like a baby bird, waiting for his kiss.

But his kisses move down my throat and across my collarbone. He nibbles my shoulder; his tongue slides over my skin, until he stops to plant a kiss in my elbow. His body presses against my legs, but then the delicious warmth moves away, and his mouth moves slowly down my arm to my wrist. He leaves a kiss in my palm that lights a fire, despite the tingling ice crystals in my stomach.

He places something in my hand and then his hair brushes the skin and I feel his warmth breath in my lap, heating the triangle between my legs. He kisses the tops of my thighs, moving down to my kneecaps. His hands lift my leg, and his mouth ends at my feet, a kiss on the bottom of each sole that sends rocket flares screaming into my head. I am about to part my legs, to lay back and pull him up over me, when he removes the tie from my eyes.

I blink. He is kneeling at my knees, a hand on either side of my thighs. I look down at the hard thing in my hand. A box. A ring box.

"Will you marry me, Hale?" he asks. He reaches out and opens the box, as I sit there staring stupidly at him. Inside, the ring sparkles with unexpected colors. There is a round diamond in the center with a blue cast to it, surrounded by a halo of purple sapphires. The filigree band twists up around the setting. I've never seen any piece of jewelry as beautiful as this.

"Will you?" Oscar asks again, removing the ring. He takes my hand, and slips the ring onto my finger. "Say yes. Please, Hale. Not just because we're supposed to, but because you think you might actually be able to fall in love with me."

"Okay," I breathe.

"Is that a yes?" he asks. I have to be able to try. He's trying hard enough for both of us and the more I'm with him, the more trouble I'm having finding reasons why I should keep fighting it. I can blame the whole arrangement on necessity, but when he talks to me, or smiles at me, or touches me, something in me keeps saying *let him*.

"Yes," I say, and Oscar jumps up, pushing me over, so he can climb on top of me, laughing. Then his mouth is on mine, and our shared laughter is caught in our kiss, with no means of escape.

#

"I want Sher to be the first one to know," I say, grabbing Oscar's arm as he tries to pull me onto my feet. He wants to go downstairs and announce my answer to Landon, even though Landon already knew about the ring. "Can I have your phone?"

"Hmm," Oscar hums, pulling the phone from his pocket. He's standing in front of me, his waist at eye level. He holds his phone just out of my reach. "I think you should earn it," he says.

"I could trade you, a present for a present," I say, but he shakes his head.

"No trades. Some things you just have to earn," he says.

"Earn how?" I ask, and he picks up the ugly tie from off the bed.

"This," he says. He holds it up, twisting the ends of the fabric around his hands, waiting for my decision. I frown, but I don't argue with him. He smiles as he slides the tie back over my eyes and around my head, knotting it carefully in the back, so it doesn't pull my hair. As he secures the knot, I smell the cologne I bought him, and feel his breath in my ear as he whispers, "Relax."

I don't bother to tell him I'm caught right in between. In the darkness that the tie provides, I feel as brave as I did on the beach, but knowing that beyond the tie, the light of the room allows him to see everything, I grow tense all over again.

"I'm going to take off my shirt, alright?" he says.

"Okay," I say. I hear the fabric as he pulls it over his head. Then, his hands are on mine, lifting my fingertips to his chest. He holds my palms against his skin as he lowers himself to kneel in front of me.

"Would you like to touch me?" he asks.

"Okay," I gulp. But he catches my hand before I can move it over his hard flesh.

"No, Hale," he whispers, leaning close to me. "Would you *like* to touch me?"

I swallow a breath. I open my eyes inside the tie, but see nothing but the dark. The brave dark. I try to forget about what can be seen beyond my own eyelashes, as I swallow again and answer, "Yes."

He lets go of my hand, and I trail the tips of my fingers over his skin. I follow the smooth arc of his collarbone, feel the rise and fall of his breath, and trace his ribs. He holds still, as I place my palm over his heart and pause to feel the beat. I work my hands outward from his hard shoulders, and down his arms, touching the taut muscles. My blood turns to liquid fire as I grasp his arms and pull him closer. I lean forward and place my lips against his skin.

His breathing escalates. He moves a hand beneath my chin, gently lifting it to reveal my lips. The pressure of his mouth against mine becomes more urgent, his tongue moving inside my cheek as his hands move down to my waist. He grips my shirt, and I put my hand on top of his to stop him. He reaches up with the opposite hand, cupping the back of my head and drawing me even closer to him.

"It's okay," he murmurs, as his mouth closes over mine again. He strips me of my shirt gently, the same way he did on the beach. But this time, he groans, laying me back on the bed, and I'm reminded that he can see everything I can't. I try to grasp the covers of the bed and yank them free to cover myself, but Oscar grabs my wrist. "No, Hale, please," he says.

I close my eyes behind the tie again and, just like at the beach, I concentrate on letting myself go. I focus on the way his hair feels, the temperature of his skin, and how he moves his mouth so that one second it feels like a massage, and the next, it sucks at my skin in a way that makes me writhe. When I do, Oscar nips at me with a chuckle.

And then his fingers are on the top button of my shorts. He unzips them and begins to peel them down.

"Wait, Oscar," I say, and he pauses, exhaling into my belly button.

"I just want to see you," he whispers. "That's all."

I try to sit up, but Oscar's hand spans out against my belly.

"What's making you nervous?" he asks. "Is it because you can't see what I'm going to do?"

"No, it's because I don't know..." I can't finish. Ugh. I hate that he asks these questions and expects me to answer out loud. I open and close my eyes under the comfortable darkness of the tie. "I don't know if I look right."

I squeeze my knees together against his chest and feel the rumble in his sternum as he laughs. He bends and plants a kiss on each of my thighs, which sets off atomic explosions all through me.

"Why would you think that?" he asks. His words vibrate through my kneecaps.

"I don't know," I say, grateful to be staring into the darkness of the tie, rather than his eyes. "It's not like I've ever compared it. But you probably will."

"Just let me look," he says, spreading more kisses over my skin as he slides his arms along the sides of my thighs. He grasps the waistband of my shorts and eases them down, along with my panties, and finally slips both off my ankles.

"I want to stop," I say. My legs, still hanging off the bed, begin to shake.

"We will," he whispers. "I promise. Right after you show me."

His hands are on my knees, moving them apart. I feel the coolness of the air suddenly close against my skin, which is the very opposite of the warmth his reassuring kiss leaves on my legs. Spread before him, I hear his satisfied groan.

"You're beautiful, Hale," he says. His breath fans across my exposed body. "You're absolutely perfect."

"I want to stop," I repeat, and the quiver from my legs is reflected in my throat.

"Alright," Oscar says. "That's all I wanted."

He guides my feet back through the legs of my panties and shorts, and slides them up toward my knees. I pull them the rest of the way, as Oscar climbs onto the bed beside me. Once my shorts are buttoned, he slips his fingers under the tie and slides it up, over my forehead.

I squint at his gentle smile. He wraps his arms around me, pulling me against his bare chest and tucking my head beneath his chin. I am grateful to nestle there, out of the direct line of his intense gaze.

"Thank you," he mumbles into my hair, as he rubs my back. "Thank you for trusting me, Hale."

I glance down at the ring on my finger, and think of how much more he's expecting me to trust him, very, very soon.

CHAPTER TWELVE

OSCAR FINALLY LEAVES ME ALONE to talk on the phone. Probably because he knows I'm still feeling kind of embarrassed, and that I really need to confide in my best friend. He lay with me a while, until things started feeling back-to-normal again, but I know the only thing that will make it feel totally okay for me is to talk to her.

"Sher?" I say into the phone.

"How's it going, Miss Fiancé?" she says, when she answers. "Is Ocker listening?"

"No," I curl up on the poufy, circular chair near the window. "He's downstairs, with his friends."

"So what's new?"

"He asked me to marry him for real, and he gave me a ring."

"Get the fuck out of here!" Sher explodes into the phone. "What's it look like? It's a rock, isn't it? Tell me exactly. I want every detail, from the 'Will you' to the 'I do'. Ok—go."

I recount what happened, and it's way more exciting to say it out loud to Sher, especially when she's cheering and shrieking at every word. I jump out of the chair, and hold up my ring to the last bit of daylight coming in through the window.

"You should see it, Sher. It's incredible," I say.

"Did you pick it out, or did he?"

"He did."

"Oh. My. God!" she swoons. "Ocker sounds sooo perfect, Hale."

Hearing her say it makes me smile. "You should see what he looks like."

"What do you mean? You said he was hot...oh, wait! Are you saying what I think you're saying? Did you do *it*?"

"No," I laugh, peeking behind me to be sure I'm still alone. I huddle over the phone and whisper to Sher, "But he stripped all the way down to his boxers, you know? Sher, you wouldn't believe his body!"

"TELL ME!" she shrieks.

"He's got muscles like you wouldn't even believe," I tell her.

"So, he stripped down," Sher says slyly. "Does that mean you did too? Don't lie now. You know I always know when you're lying."

I giggle.

"Like now. You're going to try to lie," Sher says flatly and, of course, she's right. So, I don't.

"He *looked* at me." I say, blushing, even though its just Sher I'm telling.

"There? He looked *there*?" she breaks out in wild giggles. "Did he, you know, touch you? Oh Hale, tell me every single thing—did he go down on you? Was it sexy seeing him there? What am I talking about? Of course, it's sexy! Oh man, that's the best, sexiest thing ever! Did you absolutely melt?"

"No, no, he just looked," I say. "And I don't know what he looked like, because he blindfolded me with his tie."

"Are you kidding? Holy shit, that's nuclear!" she squeals. She pauses to yell at one of her siblings who is beating on the bathroom door, begging Sher to get out. "Go away!" she shouts and then, to me, "Seriously, Hale, I'm so freakin' jealous. I want an Ocker with load of money and muscles and blindfolds. Holy shit is that hot!"

"You know what's really hot?" I whisper. "He told me it looked *beautiful*."

"Get out of here!" she shouts. "That's so *romantic!* No wonder you're marrying him. You hit the jackpot, Hale, you totally did. Tell me more about the ring!"

"It's gorgeous, Sher," I say, moving my hand back and forth to admire the sparkle. "It's got purple sapphires all around the outside and there's a big diamond in the center, but it looks like it's got this blue tint..."

"It's an infinity diamond," Oscar says from the stairs. I whirl around to see him leaning there, and the blush that's been hanging around my face all day explodes across my cheeks, until I'm sure that I look like the tip of a hot thermometer.

"How long have you been standing there?" I ask, and Oscar smiles his handsome smile.

"Long enough to know what's hot," he says.

"Ugh," I say, as Sher demands to know, from her end of the line, what's going on.

"I've gotta go Sher," I tell her. "I'll call you soon, okay?"

"Tomorrow!" she shrieks at me. "Call me tomorrow!"

"Okay, bye," I say, turning off the phone. I hold it out to Oscar, instead of taking it to him, just so I can watch him walk to me across the room. He takes the phone from my hand, then grabs my wrist and pulls me into his arms.

"Come downstairs," he says. "It's time to celebrate."

#

"We've got some news," Oscar says, when we hit the kitchen. Landon's eating canned soup at the table and Amy is painting her toenails.

"Oh yeah?" Amy twists around and holds up her foot, so we can admire her crimson toes. "What do you think?"

"Gorgeous," I say.

"I asked Hale to marry me," Oscar says. Amy drops her foot.

"Are you kidding?" she asks. I shake my head and hold up my left hand.

"Congratulations! You know, I had a little something to do with it, right? Do you like it, Hale?" Landon asks. But Amy cuts off my answer by whipping back around to face him.

"You were buying that today? While we were shopping? And you didn't tell me?"

Landon shrugs. "Oscar wanted it to be a big surprise."

"I bet he did," she says sourly. She turns back to us, but it's Oscar that she pins with her glare. "Don't you think it's a little soon? You were still with Sophia last week. You were Mr. Loyalty, remember, OC?"

"I do," Oscar replies evenly. "I don't know why I need to explain this to you, Amy, but I found the girl I want to marry and I'm not letting her get away."

"Yeah, hon, what are you getting so riled up about?" Landon asks.

"You don't think it's a little rushed?"

"It's not my business," Landon shrugs. I shift anxiously beside Oscar, and he drapes an arm around my shoulders.

I was hoping for too much. I hoped that Amy would gush and shriek and want to inspect the ring, like Sher would if she were here, and that Landon would clap Oscar on the back, and they'd shake hands and break out something to toast with. But I didn't think we'd get totally slammed for rushing, or that it'd be followed up with an 'it's not my business' chaser.

"If you thought Sophia was flipping before, just wait." Amy says. "Are you gonna make me be the one to break it to her? Because I'm sorry, OC, but I'll have to totally make you sound like an ass."

Oscar frowns. I'm sure he didn't expect it to go this way either.

"No, I'll tell her," he says. "But thanks for celebrating with us and making the night so special."

"Whoa now," Landon says, rising from the table. "You're absolutely right, OC. My best buddy is only getting married once— God willing—and this is the night to celebrate it! This isn't about Sophia; it's about Oscar and Hale. Congrats, Hale! Come here and give me a hug! Let's have a drink and hope it stays in me! What've we got to drink, OC?"

"I have a bottle of champagne and then it's beer from there on out," Oscar laughs.

"It's all champagne tonight!" Landon says. "Alright, buddy, bring on the toast!"

Landon catches me up in a big bear hug, and Oscar pulls the champagne from the fridge. Amy, however, just screws the cap on her nail polish. When Landon releases me, and we're almost left face-to-face, she pushes a smile across her face and says, "Congrats, Hale. I guess the best girl won."

It's like she's stomping on all the warmth and budding friendship we had going at the mall. Her glare makes me feel like I should apologize, but all I want to do is punch her in her big, sour face.

"I wasn't trying to steal him," I say. "I'm sorry about Sophia, but it wasn't like I did anything on purpose. This just—happened. I was surprised too."

"Lighten up, babe," Landon tells Amy from across the room. "Let it go. This is supposed to be a party! Sophia'll be fine. You don't have to fight her battles."

Amy seems to snap out of it. She lifts her chin and gives Landon a smile. "I'm not," she says. She lifts my hand in hers to take a look at the ring. She flashes me an attempt at an apologetic smile. "This isn't earning me a place in the bridal party, is it? I am happy for you. I just wish things had happened differently."

I don't say *me too* this time. I don't really want to let her off the hook, but I'm not good at holding a grudge either. And this is Oscar's best friend's girlfriend. We're probably going to be seeing a lot of each other, and it'd be nice if things could get back to the way they were at the mall.

She looks at the ring and gives me a feather-light embrace.

"Congratulations," she says, then walks away to get the cup that Landon holds out for her.

CHAPTER THIRTEEN

A COUPLE HOURS LATER, LANDON is smashed. So smashed that he spends ten minutes trying to get out one sentence, but he keeps cracking up in the middle and then he starts over at the beginning and tries again. When Oscar turns his phone back on, it starts ringing almost non-stop, and Landon starts parroting after every single ring, "You gonna get that?" until Oscar switches it off again.

"Who is it?" I ask, and he frowns like he doesn't want to tell me, but he does.

"Sophia," he says.

I haven't drunk anything but a couple sips of the champagne. I still feel a little sick about what happened with Amy and Landon, and I think Oscar might feel the same, because he hasn't gone back for more to drink either. But Landon is taking care of most of it, and Amy is right behind him. Twice, she's ambled over, sloshed her beer on me, and told me how she *wants* to be happy for us, she really does. All I want to do is sneak away and call Sher, so I can feel happy again.

"I know," Amy announces. "I want to go swimming! Who wants to see my new bikini? It's red—red—like my toes."

She stumbles over to the shopping bags strewn across the Inflato-mattress and stuffs her arm into one of the bigger bags.

"I'll wear this!" she says, pulling what looks like a lot of red string, with a couple red knee patches attached, from the bag.

"I'll watch," Landon says, stumbling over, as Amy grabs her shirt and peels it off. She's not wearing a bra.

"I'm almost naked!" she laughs, as Landon shouts at her that everyone's looking. Oscar shields his eyes with a hand on his brow, peeking at me from underneath with a *wow, I can't believe she's that drunk* grin. But then Amy peels off her shorts too and she twirls them, like helicopter blades, over her head.

"Put on clothes!" Landon bellows at her.

"Alright, alright," she snaps, but it takes her twice as long as it should to figure out how to get the bikini on. When Landon sees that we're not looking at his naked girlfriend, he sidles over to her and gets tangled in her bikini strings, laughing and mumbling things that are uncomfortably loud enough to hear.

"Let's go outside," Oscar says. "We can sit on the beach and make sure they don't drown themselves."

We go out to the beach, but even though Oscar switches on the floodlights at the back door and at the top of the house, they don't quite reach the part of the beach where the dock extends out. It's not pitch black tonight, though, and the moonlight sparkles on the water.

We sit on the sand, and Oscar says, "This isn't the engagement party I wanted us to have."

" Amy's really mad. And I don't think Landon agrees with how fast it's all happening."

"Landon is worried that we'll jump into this and jump right back out. He knows something is strange about how I met you, but he can't figure it all out, and he's frustrated that I'm not telling him everything. But I don't think we should include anyone else. Secrets still have a way of leaking out. Even with the strongest friendship, you never know if it'll still be intact a year from now. And if, a year from now, a friend might think your secret isn't that big of a deal anymore, so why keep it. That's how things come to the surface."

"I'm not telling anyone else. Not even Sher." I say. I don't mention that it makes me feel sick inside to keep anything from her, especially when I need help figuring out what to do.

"Good," Oscar says. He looks over his shoulder toward the beach house. "I wonder if they're even going to come out here."

Just then, I hear the back door slam and Landon's insane laughter, withAmy barking at him to stop pulling on her bikini strings. They stumble their way down the path to us.

"We're gonna go skinny dippin'" Amy says. Her bikini is totally messed up, but at least it's covering all the necessary parts.

"*In* our clothes," Landon adds.

"No, you're gonna go chunky dunkin' *in your clothes*." Amy corrects him. Landon looks down at himself and nods in agreement.

"Nobody's going swimming tonight," Oscar says. Both friends stare at him, confused, and I think they're both trying to compute. Oscar adds, "There's a shark warning up."

"Sharks?" Amy asks, peering out across the dark water. "I don't see any sharks."

"Sharks!" Landon howls. "This is tap water! Not an ocean!"

"And you're 10 bananas drunk, buddy," Oscar says, holding up both hands with his fingers outstretched.

"I'm not 10 bananas," Landon says. "Not yet."

"Oh, you're at least 10 bananas," Oscar says.

"What's 10 bananas?" I ask.

"When you hold up your hands to try and count your fingers, but all you see are bananas and all you can think of is how hungry you are."

"Really? Ten?" Landon asks and then he breaks out in such a fit of laughter that he falls over, rolling on the sand at Amy's feet. She kicks sand on him.

"Is there sharks or isn't there?" she snaps.

"Sharks, yes," Oscar tells her, but she narrows her eyes at him.

"You're lying," she says.

"No swimming tonight," Oscar repeats. A sly smile spreads across Amy's face, as she plays with one of the bikini strings dangling at her hip.

"What are you going to do about it?" she says.

"I don't know," Oscar tells her. "Hope you don't drown?"

Amy starts off for the beach, calling over her shoulder, "Are you gonna save me? Gimme a shark bite of your own?"

Oscar stays seated, even as Amy nears the water's edge. She peeks over her shoulder to see if he's coming. She slows down, and the excitement drains out of her. She walks in, only ankle deep, and kicks up the water.

Landon jumps up and heads for her, his thumbs in his waistband.

"We can dip at the edge!" he calls to her.

"Please don't!" Oscar shouts after him. Landon reaches the edge, but he doesn't make a move to strip. Oscar and I just laugh. With his eye still on his drunk friends, he says to me, "I was thinking we'd get married when we get back. We can have a chapel wedding. You could tell Sher to buy her dress and we'll get yours when we go home."

Home. When we go home. He's obviously not talking about my, and my dad's, apartment. I run my thumb over the back of my ring band and get overwhelmed again, thinking of how everything is going to change. Even though living with my father has never been perfect, he's still the only one I've ever lived with. I don't know if we'll live near my dad and Sher; if I'll ever be able to go to college; what a life with Oscar really means. We've never talked about that, beyond cooking, cleaning, being good in bed, and now it doesn't feel like a good trade at all.

"Why do we have to rush? Don't you know I'm trustworthy by now? I'm not going to tell anybody anything, Oscar."

"I know you won't," he says. I watch him struggle to say the next part. "But we don't know if your father would, Hale. I don't want to hurt your feelings, but with your dad's drinking problem..."

"You think a marriage certificate is going to shut him up when he's on a bender?" I ask. I'm less offended than I am embarrassed. My father's drinking has corroded so much of our lives that it's gotten to be a dark spot I just try to keep hidden. When it is brought out into the light, it is so much worse, and less easily explained than: 'he just drinks a little too much sometimes'. It's a whole storm that rips through our lives, dumping our money, and chipping away at our family name every single time he goes to the bar.

"I don't think it will prevent everything that could happen," Oscar says. "But I think it might help him think twice about it, if we're all on the same page. He's talked to my father about entering rehab. My father's offered him full treatment, and your dad accepted the help. He's trying, Hale. He's trying hard. He doesn't want to mess this up for himself or for us. It's obvious what you mean to him, and I still think that will outride his love of alcohol."

"Fat chance of that," I snort. "He threw me out to *marry a stranger*. If you're putting all your hopes on my dad's love for me, I think you're asking for a lot."

There's a whoop from the water's edge that draws our eyes up. Landon's staggered a ways down the dock, past the red post. He clunks into the railing, and the whole dock quivers. Grabbing hold of the post he shouts, "Whoa!"

"I better go get him," Oscar says. "One wrong step and he's either going over, or dropping through, the bottom of that hand rail."

Oscar hops up and jogs down the dock toward Landon. Amy, still at the water's edge, calls to me.

"Come 'ere, Haley! Come 'ere and put your feet in with me! The water's sooo warm!" She slips and falls on her butt. When she stands back up, her boob plops right out of her bikini top.

"Amy, your top!" I shout, motioning to her wardrobe malfunction. All she does is cup her ear with one hand.

"What?" she shouts.

"Your top! Your boob!" I shout again, but it's no use. The wind is coming off the water so even though it sounds like she's standing next to me when she talks, she still can't hear a thing I'm screaming at her. She shrugs, oblivious, boob flapping as she kicks along the water. I get up to dust the sand off my butt, and catch sight of Amy as she whirls around at the sharp sound of a splash.

I search the dock, trying to put together what I hear with what I see. The handrail is intact, but Landon is bobbing in the water. A frightened howl comes out of him, as Oscar pulls off his shoes and vaults the rail into the water.

"Holy shit!" Amy shrieks. "Landon's drowning! Hale! Landon's drowning!"

I get to the water's edge and Amy grabs my hand as we watch Oscar surface by himself, catch a breath, and dive under again. Amy drags me with her to the edge of the dock, but I dig in my heels.

"I can't!" I shout as she tugs my hand.

"Come on!" she screams. "We got to help them!"

"I can't swim!"

But Amy's got a vice grip on my wrist, and she yanks me out onto the planks of the dock. She drags me along with her, as I shriek for her to stop and let go. She doesn't.

"Help me," she roars.

"I can't swim!" I scream at her. I sit and Amy gives me such a hard tug that I fall forward on my face. She drags me along, the water sloshing just under the planks, and my blood freezing in my veins. I try to get to my feet, to hang on as we pass one of the yellow-marked posts.

Oscar drags Landon up to the surface. Landon sputters and chokes. Oscar shouts, "I got him!" He side-strokes toward the shore, hanging onto Landon.

But Amy doesn't let go. And she's laughing.

I'm white-hot screaming, trying to cling to the passing beams, but Amy yanks and pulls and drags me along. We pass the red post as Oscar swims in the other direction.

"What are you doing? Let go!" I shout. "I can't swim! I CAN'T SWIM!"

"Amy! Let go of her!" Oscar shouts, but he's doing everything he can to keep both his and Landon's heads, above water. I see him struggling to pull Landon through the water even faster.

"Stop! STOP!" I holler. Amy lets go, but she turns on me like a rabid dog.

"You're going in!" Amy laughs. "Least you can do is take a dunk. God knows I got soaked…"

She swoops down, her nose centimeters from mine. I grab hold of a post as I scream back at her, "What are you talking about?"

"He was mine!" Amy shrieks. She grabs hold of my fingers, prying them backward off the post.

"He's still yours! Oscar's trying to help him, don't you get it?"

"Mine?" she grunts. Every time she gets one hand loose, I wrap the other arm around the post. Oscar pauses to look over his shoulder, and then resumes at a clip toward the shore, towing Landon with him.

Not getting anywhere, Amy jumps up and grabs my hair. She pulls backward so hard; I can't help but let go. It feels like she's ripping my head in half. She drags me away from the post as I try to stop her from scalping me.

"He was supposed to be mine!" she barks. "But he picked Sophia. They should've been over! Rick was gonna make sure…"

"Rick?" I shriek. "You sent Rick after Oscar?"

I see the rage roll over her as she realizes her mistake. The answer she gives me is pulling her leg back and firing it at me, hitting me in the side. I grunt with the impact and fall backward. Amy leans down and punches me in the face.

"Time to go swimming, bitch," she growls, digging her fingernails into my arm. I'm rigid with fear of the water, and my temple throbs. Groping for a post to hang onto, my eye begins to pulse with the pain as she jerks me toward the edge of the dock. I'm going to die. I glimpse Oscar dragging Landon onto the shore and get hold of a post. I cling to it and the whole dock begins to shake, as Amy tries to tear my grip loose and push me in. She's going to throw me in, and I'm going to die. I shut my eyes and hold tight, screaming.

"Get away from her!" Oscar's voice cuts through the noise. Amy shrieks as he wrenches her hands from me. Oscar grabs her and throws her over the side of the handrail. She screams, and lands with a splash.

Oscar tips my face up to him and growls, "What did she do to you?" He sucks in a breath as he scans over my face.

I hear Amy cursing and splashing around in the water, and I think I'm going to throw up. My head is throbbing in the back and in the front, and I want to stay where I am, curled on the dock, even though the sound of Amy's splashing petrifies me. Oscar lifts me into his arms and I whimper.

"She knew," I whisper to him. "She knew Rick Tatum."

Amy flails toward the shore, howling from the water, "I'm gonna drown! Landon! Help me, I'm gonna drown!"

Landon stands unsteadily, at the end of the dock as Oscar steps off, and Amy washes up on the shore. She crawls out, coughing.

Oscar's voice vibrates through his chest as he shouts at her, "You better stay the hell away from me, Amy! All your shit will be on the front lawn in about ten seconds, and you can walk home for all I care!"

"Nooo," she howls after him. "I'm sorry! I didn't mean it! I was just drunk..."

But Oscar carries me up to the house, and Landon follows us inside.

"Are you okay, Hale?" Landon asks, even though he doesn't sound okay himself. Oscar lays me down on the couch, and when he flips on a light, Landon gets a look at my face and breathes, "Holy shit."

Since my left temple seems to have it's own heartbeat, I figure it's got to be pretty bad, even though I can still see fine out of it. Oscar brings a bag of frozen peas, which makes me yelp when he applies them.

Amy lifts the latch on the back door, and Landon storms her. "Out! I saw Hale's face! What the hell is the matter with you?" he yells. Startled, she lets go of the door handle, and Landon yanks the door shut, throwing the lock. "Stay the fuck out!"

Landon's veins rise up on his forehead as he crosses the room to the inflato-bed. He grabs armloads of Amy's things and shoots across the living room to the front door. He swings it open so hard that the knob hits the wall. Once outside, he whips Amy's things off to the side of the driveway. Something shatters, and pair of her panties catches on a shrub branch.

Amy appears as Landon's hauling out a second load of her things. He dumps her bag, and tosses her shopping bags at her feet while she shrieks at him. I don't think Landon says a word. He comes back inside and slams the door.

"Sorry about the door, buddy," he grumbles, and Oscar says, "No problem."

Landon stomps into the bathroom and slams that door shut too. I watch as Amy gathers her stuff. She sighs, she kicks things, and finally, she piles it all up beside Landon's cars and sits on his trunk.

"She can't walk home in the dark," I say. I'm not being sympathetic. I'm trying to figure out the fastest way to get her gone.

"I know," Oscar says, as the bathroom door swings open. Landon comes out and grabs his keys.

"I'm driving her back to wherever there's a bus," Landon says. "Where's a bus?"

"Town," Oscar says. "You sure you should be driving?"

"I'm fine," Landon grumbles. Oscar gives Landon the directions, and Landon grabs his keys and heads out the door. He tells Amy to get the fuck off his trunk, but otherwise, the two don't talk. Land gets into the driver's seat and just pops the trunk as he starts the car. In the glow of the taillights, Amy loads her stuff into the trunk alone. When she's done, she slides into the passenger's seat, and Landon's back tires spout gravel and sand as they take off down the driveway.

Oscar sits down beside me on the couch. He runs his fingers over the back of my head. I wince. "She got you back there too?"

I nod. He gets up, and comes back with a bag of frozen green beans this time. The peas are still on my face. He puts the beans on the back of my head. It feels like I'm caught inside an ice cube tray.

"We use more of our groceries for injuries than eating," I try to joke. Oscar tries to laugh, but it only comes out as a puff of air.

"You said Amy mentioned Rick Tatum?" he asks.

"She said she sent him after you."

"Damn it," he says. "I thought she might have been the one."

"You did?"

"Yeah," he groans. "But I never thought she'd go so far. Amy was always telling me things that Sophia was saying and doing, while we were apart. I thought Amy just had my back. But then, a couple weeks ago, Amy came onto me while we were all hanging out

MISTY PROVENCHER

together at the bar. A huge group of all our friends were there, and Amy caught me by the bathrooms. She told me Sophia was cheating on me and tried to kiss me, but I just figured she was wasted. I was so mad about what she was telling me about Soph, I just ignored what she did."

I take a deep breath. He sounds heartbroken, as if, maybe, he really had loved Sophia, and it was only the lies Amy told him that had gotten in the way. Maybe every problem they ever had was all because of Amy. My mind jumps from one thought to another to another. What if it's true? What if he realizes he's stuck with me, but really wants her after all?

"But if she was the one that sent Tatum, than she'd know he's dead."

"I would think so too," Oscar says, and I shiver.

"Then she's a psychopath."

"Something's definitely wrong with her."

Headlights shine in through the front windows.

"Land couldn't have gotten her into town that quick," Oscar says, rising off the couch. He shields his eyes from the oncoming glare. "Who is that?"

CHAPTER FOURTEEN

THE CAR SPINS INTO THE OPEN spot on the opposite side of Oscar's truck. Oscar walks to the front windows and peering out, he says, "What is she doing here?"

Sophia skitters up to the front door.

"Hi," she says through the screen. Her voice is high-pitched and funny, like she's trying to be cordial while being chased with a chainsaw. Her eyes dart around the room. "I don't see Landon's car. Are he and Amy here?"

"They left," Oscar says. "What are you doing here?"

Sophia suddenly grabs the handle of the door and rushes in. "We don't have time, Oscar," she begins at a rapid-fire pace. "I've been calling—there's something wrong. Amy's flipped out. She sent a guy after you."

"I know," Oscar says. "We just found that out."

"You did? Somebody came after you?"

"Not up here," Oscar says carefully. "Probably couldn't find me."

"Thank God," Sophia says. "Where's Amy now? I've got a few things to say to her."

"Landon took her to the bus stop in town. She tried to hurt Hale."

"Are you kidding? What did she do?" Sophia turns to look at me, seeing me on the couch for the first time. I lower the bag of peas and Sophia gasps. "She doesn't need to be on a bus. She needs to be in a psych ward."

I see the concern shoot across Oscar's face and disappear. We can't call the cops. If Amy tells them about Rick Tatum, then the police might eventually be able to trace it back to our fathers being at the bar where Tatum died. Oscar rubs his chin.

"No, I think she's just really mixed up right now," he says, but it doesn't even sound like he believes it. "She got thrown out of here, and Landon's furious with her. A ride home on the bus might be what she needs."

"You think she needs time to clear her head?" Sophia squeaks. She narrows her eyes on Oscar. "She beat up your girlfriend and sent a guy after you. Why are you defending her?"

"I'm not," he says. "I just think she's being overly protective of you, and she took it too far. I didn't want to involve the cops since she's your friend."

Sophia's tongue rolls in her cheek. She gives Oscar a hard glare, like his face is a puzzle that she's putting together. "You *did* her, didn't you?"

"What?" Oscar's eyes bulge. "What are you talking about?"

"She said you almost did it." Sophia says. "She said that you came onto her, and she held back because of me. I didn't believe her. I thought she was really going crazy, but it's true, isn't it?"

"I'm sorry," Oscar says. He glances in my direction with a tiny shake of his head. That's how I know he's lying. "I'm so sorry it had to come out like this."

Then he turns his head to me, confirming the lie with a wink that Sophia doesn't see. Her arms drop at her sides.

"Are you kidding me?" she says. "You wanted to cheat on me with Amy? With my best friend?"

"She didn't tell you the whole truth," Oscar says. "It wasn't me coming on to her. Amy has been hitting on me since we met. You've seen it yourself, Soph. You've made jokes about it before.

"Amy kept showing up at my house all the time, and you know how she kept calling my phone when we finally got to go out on a date alone. But last week, she showed up at my house and told me that you were cheating on me. Things hadn't been going right with us. You know that. I figured, for once, Amy was telling the truth. It made sense at the time. I made the mistake of believing her, and I cheated on you. I think we both got screwed, and I'm really sorry."

Sophia stands there blankly, trying to process what Oscar is telling her.

"I hate you," she says, then she turns to me. "You should get away from him. Do you hear this? He's a liar and a cheat. He'll do the same to you."

"No, he won't," I say, dropping the bag of peas on the couch. "I've got too much on him."

"Then you deserve whatever you get," Sophia says. "Have a happy fucking life, Oscar."

And she storms out the door, runs to her car, and guns it down the drive into the night.

#

"Paid for Crazy Cakes to get on the bus, so she'll be back in the vicinity of home in a couple hours," Landon says when he returns. He's throwing his stuff into his bag as he talks. "As for me, I think I'm just going to head back tonight, if you don't mind. The birthday weekend is kind of a bust."

"Stick around," Oscar says. "It's not your birthday yet. We can still have a good time."

"Nah, I think I've had all I can take. I'm going to head home."

"A few minutes earlier and you could've carpooled with Sophia," Oscar says.

"What? She was up here again?"

"Yeah. To warn us about Amy. I don't know why she didn't just call you."

"You've got to be kidding," Landon groans. "She didn't call me, because Amy said she was acting nutty and screaming about you. I didn't want to hear it, so I blocked her calls."

"What a mess," Oscar says.

"Yeah buddy." Landon says. He hauls the strap of his bag onto his shoulder. "Well, okay, I'm out. You two have a good rest of the weekend, alright?"

Once he's gone, Oscar locks the doors and insists I lie on the couch with the peas on my eye. He carefully checks the back of my head, before I do. It's sore from the hair pulling, but he reports there aren't any bumps or cuts. I lay back, and he lifts my shirt up, just over my stomach, pressing along my side gingerly with his fingertips, and asking if anything hurts. It's a little sore, but nothing bad.

"I still can't believe she did that," he says. "I would've liked to do the same to her."

"But you didn't," I say.

"I don't hit girls," he says. "I do throw them in the lake, though."

I close my eyes a moment, and Oscar says, "Lift your head. You can rest it in my lap."

I do as he says, with a pillow between my head and his legs. I stare up at him.

"What are you going to do, if the whole story about cheating with Amy gets back to Landon?" I ask. Oscar's eyes travel thoughtfully across the room.

"I hate lying to him, but I guess I'll have to deny it, and rely on Amy's boatload of crazy for credibility," Oscar says. "But I'm hoping it doesn't come up."

"Me too," I agree quietly.

"Something else on your mind?" he asks.

"I was wondering," I begin, and bite my lip. He puts a hand on my knee, his head tipped down and his eyes searching for mine, like an incredibly handsome, but inquisitive, puppy. He waits for my answer. "Did you say all of that to Sophia because you wanted to be sure she wouldn't come back, or because you meant it?"

"Both," he says. "You're still wondering if I'm in love with Sophia?"

I drop my eyes away from his. "Yes."

"I told you before that she's not even on my radar anymore. Nothing's changed."

"Yes it has. Amy drove wedges between you. It sounds like she told a lot of lies on both sides to tear you two apart. You obviously loved Sophia once. Maybe, if there hadn't been any interference, you still would."

"I never loved Sophia," he says. "I liked her. That's why I dated her. But I never fell in love with Sophia. I'm sure things would've turned out different if Amy had never been involved, but would it have worked out with Sophia and me? I don't know and I don't care. I found the person I want to be with. I'm not questioning that."

"But you have to marry me."

"I don't *have to* do anything."

"You said you did."

"I said I'm loyal, and that I would do anything to help my father."

"Including marrying me," I say, sitting up beside him.

"Hale," Oscar says. His gaze filters out everything else in the room. "I want this."

His eyes are warm and reassuring. I want to believe every word. I touch the ring band on my finger, and he notices. He puts his hand on mine.

"I want you so much," he says. "I've never felt like this about anyone else. Not even close. You have this way, Hale, I don't know how to describe it, but you have this way about you that I can't resist. When we're apart, it's like I find these little holes in myself. Holes I can't fill up on my own. Things are missing and the longer I'm away from you, the more clear and deep those holes become. But then you walk into the room, and everything comes back together for me again. All my emptiness is filled in. I can't resist you, Hale, because I need you so much. Without you, I'm not even me."

I climb into his lap, taking his face between my hands, and guiding his mouth to my kiss. This time, it is my tongue that searches for his, and my hands that find the edge of his shirt, peeling it up, over his head. A deep moan grows from inside his throat. I slide a knee on either side of his thighs and deepen our kiss, pressing to him, until the sound of his pleasure vibrates against my lips.

Oscar reciprocates. He wraps his arms around me, sliding his hands up my back, and grips my shoulders, pulling me down against him. My knees spread even wider and I feel his desire growing stronger as our kiss intensifies. He exhales, hot and fast, across my cheek as he arches to press himself more tightly to me. I pull back and he stops.

"Did I hurt you?" he asks.

"No," I say. "I just..." How do I say I panicked, feeling him between my legs? It's stupid. It's not like we're even naked. He's only half naked, and I'm not at all naked, but I'm still panicking, *feeling* the fact that he wants to do *it*. He catches my lip between his teeth.

"No," he pleads in a whisper. "Don't ask me to stop this time, Hale. Please don't."

I don't want him to stop, but I'm afraid to go any further. I know how sex works, I've read books that explained it, but now that I'm sitting in his lap, there are too many variables. The worst being, I don't know what I'm supposed to do. We aren't married. I'm not on The Pill or anything. He told me he wants me to be good in bed, and I don't have a clue how to do that. I'm afraid he's going to be completely turned off by my total ignorance, when we actually do *it*.

I move to swing my leg onto the floor, but Oscar grabs my hips, pulling me back down to him. He lays his head back, looking up at the ceiling.

"I'll stop," he says, "but you've got to talk to me. I need to know how to make you comfortable with this. You want to be married before we do this, is that it?"

"I guess," I say. I'd say anything to escape it right now.

"I don't have a problem with that," Oscar says. "We don't have to have sex yet. But can I touch you? Can we do anything else?"

"I don't know," I blush, looking into my lap, which means I'm also looking into his too. He feels so good against me; I don't want to stop. But I'm scared to go further.

"Hey," he says, lifting my chin so our eyes meet. His are so dark and deep. I don't want to stop. How do I say I don't want to stop, without saying I want to keep going? "I'm asking you to make the rules. I promise not to cross the line, but I need you to tell me where the line is."

And the words slip out. "I don't want to stop."

Oscar smiles. "That's okay too," he laughs softly. He lifts my hand with his enormous ring on it. "You see this ring? That means I'm staying. That means you belong to me. And by accepting it that ring also means you're staying and that I belong to you. We can wait until we're married, if it makes you comfortable. Or we can have sex before we're married, and that's okay too. We belong to each other, Hale, and sex or no sex, nothing's going to change that."

"I'm scared that it's going to hurt," I say. Oscar nods, like he's absorbing my words.

"It probably will," he says. "But only the first time. After that, it should feel good. But for our first time, we'll go very slow and I'll be as careful as I can."

"Okay," I say. My eyes fill up, but it's not all from nerves. Oscar chuckles again.

"If you're okay, than what's the matter?"

"You said..." I start to cry. Oscar tries to comfort me, rubbing my back and whispering, "Shhh, it's okay. Whatever it is, it's okay, Hale."

"You said you wanted me to cook and clean and." I begin to hiccup and can't finish.

"Oh no," Oscar says with a smile. "I said you needed to be good in bed. That's what you're worried about?"

I nod.

"Hale, this is all new to you, I get that," he says. "I don't expect you to know what you're doing at first. In fact, I'm glad you don't."

"But what if I'm never good at it?"

"You will be. I'm not worried about that," he says. My head begins to throb a little and I put my hand to my temple. Oscar lays his hand gently on mine. "Is it hurting again?"

"Yes," I say.

"Let's do this," he says. "I'm going to get you some aspirin and get you up to bed. We don't need to talk anymore about this tonight."

Oscar lets go of me, and we both get up from the couch. He twines his arm around my waist and we walk upstairs together. A bed has never looked as good as this one looks now. He deposits me at the side, and I perch on the edge.

"I'm going to grab that aspirin," he says. He jogs downstairs and brings back water and medicine before I can even kick off my shoes. I swallow down the pill he gives me. Oscar moves the shopping bags off the bed, but picks up the nightgown I bought.

"Do you want to wear this to bed?" he asks. My head is going *bomp bomp bomp* and he wants me to get into a nightgown. And getting into a nightgown means getting out of clothes, but it's that middle naked part that usually leads to trouble.

"I can sleep in this."

"I'm not going to jump you, Hale," he says, and without waiting for an answer, he lifts off my shirt. Almost without blinking, he removes my bra and slides the lime-green fabric down over my head. "Stand up a second," he says and when I do, he reaches under my gown to hook his fingers into my shorts. He slides them off, along with my panties, and smoothes down my gown, before pulling back the covers on the bed.

The rain starts then, soft drops on the skylight. I lie down, and the pillow feels cool and good.

"I have another present for you," I say, as Oscar unbuttons his shorts.

"Another?"

I nod and point to the shopping bags he's put on the chair. "The big one."

Oscar gets the bag. He opens it and pulls out the pajama bottoms I bought him. He holds them up with a grin.

"I'll wear a pair tonight," he says. "But just so you know, I usually don't allow clothes in my bed. They're bad for the atmosphere I like to create."

I giggle and clasp my head, closing my eyes as he removes his boxers and slips on the bottoms I bought him. He climbs into bed as the rain kicks up. He turns me away from him and curls up against my back.

"Go to sleep," he whispers, leaving a kiss on my neck. I drift off to sleep, listening to the rhythm of the raindrops overhead.

CHAPTER FIFTEEN

OSCAR GENTLY SHAKES ME AWAKE. The moon is hanging above the skylight, blurred by the rain, and the faux bedside candles are flickering.

"What's the matter?" I ask.

"Nothing," Oscar says. "Just need to wake you up every few hours to be sure you don't have a concussion."

"I'm awake, so I guess I don't."

"How's your head?"

"I think it's okay."

"Do you want some more aspirin?"

"No thanks."

We lie on our backs, looking up at the mirrors over our heads. "You can go back to sleep," Oscar says. I try to close my eyes, but I'm wide-awake now and every time I look up, I see the outline of Oscar's powerful body under the sheet. Then I see him looking back at me.

"The rain is really coming down," I say. "Have you been awake long?"

"I haven't gone to sleep," he says. "I wanted to keep an eye on you. I went through all my phone messages though."

"Sophia?"

"Mostly," he says. "But my father called too. He said that the news reported that there is going to be an autopsy done on Tatum. They're reporting that there aren't any leads. They still suspect foul play because of how he hit his head, but they want to rule out the possibility of drugs. If he has drugs in his system, they might assume it was a drug deal that went bad."

"I hope they find drugs," I say, and immediately feel the heavy mixture of guilt and hope drop into my stomach.

"If they do, it would put my father at ease. But if he was on drugs, the whole thing with Amy is even more haywire," Oscar says. He slides his arm beneath my pillow, and in the mirror overhead, I watch his muscles ripple as he moves closer beneath the sheet. The rain taps even harder on the skylight. "But there's no point in worrying about any of it right now. Nothing we can do about it."

"I guess not," I say, and my stomach jumps as Oscar's hand grazes over it. "What are you doing?"

"Nothing. Just touching you," he says innocently. "That's okay, isn't it?"

"It's okay," I say, as some thunder rumbles in the distance.

"Storm's coming," he whispers.

"I used to hate storms when I was little," I tell him. "I used to hide between my parents in their bed, even though my mom would try to send me back to my own bed."

"Your mom would?"

"Yeah, she would." I say. "But my dad would always let me stay. I think he was just as scared as I was."

Oscar chuckles at that, and his hand returns to cup my stomach. "Would you kick our children out of our bed, or let them stay?"

"Children?" I gulp. Children. He didn't even just say child. He said children. I've never once thought about having children. That's always something that happened to older people, during parts of life that were too distant for me to worry about. But now, Oscar's put the idea front and center, and it makes me feel like I'm in the front row of a movie theater, tipping my head back and trying to make sense of this new, bigger picture.

"I want children, don't you?" he says.

"No," I say quickly. "Not now. Not soon. Maybe not ever."

Oscar just laughs. "You've got time to think about it."

"What if I never want to have kids? What if the answer is never?"

"I'd be disappointed," Oscar says.

"You don't think I'd be disappointed?" I squeak, pushing him away. "Never getting to go to college, or have career, or a life of my own? You don't think it'd be disappointing to just sit home, squeezing out baby after baby, while you're off doing...I don't even know what you'd be doing!"

"I work with my father," he says. "Financial investments."

I pull back the sheet and sit up, so I can tower over him. "So, while you're off, having a life, you want to trap me at home with a screaming, whining football team? And you can't see how I'd be disappointed?"

Oscar's stomach muscles jump when he laughs. "I don't think it'd be like that at all, Hale. You can have your career. We could have a nanny."

"You'd let some stranger raise your children?" I snap. "If we had children, there's no way someone else would be raising them. That's ridiculous."

" I'm glad you're thinking about it, at least," Oscar says.

"I'm thinking you're nuts," I say. The wind picks up and the branch-women, outside, wave their arms, throwing frantic shadows against the wall. The thunder rumbles even closer, and a flash of lightening startles me as it illuminates the room. Oscar's hand is on my wrist, pulling me back down into his arms. He throws a leg over both of mine.

"I think you're still just a little scared of the unknown," he says, tipping my face toward the ceiling as he kisses down the side of my cheek. I watch him do it, mesmerized by the way the cut of his jaw looks, as his mouth moves along my skin. I turn my face toward him, to return his kiss, but under his breath he mumbles, "No, no. Just watch," as he gently pushes away my lips.

I look up into the mirror, and watch as his leg releases me and his hand passes beneath the sheet. He pulls it from me, and goose bumps rise up across my chest, not from the temperature of the room, but from how close he is. From what he is going to do.

His lips move down my neck as he slips a hand beneath the silk bodice of my gown. My nipples rise up to the warm ceiling of his palm. A shock of lightening flashes overhead, momentarily blinding me.

But his fingertips are soft on my stomach, making their way down my side to finally rest at the top of my thigh. I let my gaze drift downward, but the moment I do, Oscar whispers into my hair, "Are you watching, Hale?"

As I look up, his head lowers to my breast, taking my nipple into his mouth. Streaks of lightening course through me, and Oscar's tongue vibrates deliciously with his low rumble of pleasure. I close my eyes and then, as if it is punishment for doing so, Oscar's lips close around me and he gives the point of my breast a sharp tug.

My eyes flick back to the ceiling reflection of his long fingers, as he gathers up my gown in his palm.

"Yes," I answer.

"Good."

I swallow, as he continues to ease up the fabric until I am exposed from the waist down. One of his hands slides between my legs, drifting a finger lightly down the inside of my thigh. My knees jerk apart with the tickle.

"Good," Oscar chuckles, the sound as low and deep as the thunder. He leans over me, the muscles of his back flexing, as his dark hair moves over my stomach. He kisses the bottom of my sternum, the soft upper part of my belly, and slips his tongue into my navel. I giggle, and Oscar smothers his laugh in kisses that make a crescent moon shape around my belly button. He leans across my leg, peeking between my knees, and his pleasurable groan rumbles against my thigh. I feel his breath, hot and warm, as he shifts his body weight, easing his torso between my knees.

I tense as Oscar spreads my legs further apart, wiggling between them.

"Let me," he whispers, and when he catches me looking down at him, he smiles and moves his gaze up to the ceiling, in reminder. I lay back again and stare into the overhead mirror as his head dips between my thighs. At first, I curl my toes, embarrassed, but then his breathe steams against my opened flesh, and his moist finger moves between my folds. A moan rips from my chest.

In the strikes of lightening, I watch Oscar lift his finger to his mouth, sucking it before he drops his hand back down between my thighs and slowly eases it back into me. The tip of his finger caresses me deeper and deeper. He lowers his mouth against me, and at the same time, my body takes over, trembling against the mattress. Oscar spreads the palm of his free hand against my stomach, but he doesn't stop. He swirls his tongue against me, and the involuntary begging breaks through my lips, one plead after another, as he slips a second finger inside me, gently stretching me even wider.

"Does that feel good?" he asks, and I breathe my answer. He nips the inside of my thigh as he withdraws his fingers. He slips off the pajama bottoms I gave him, dropping them off the end of the bed. In the reflection, I stare down at the hard cords of his shoulders, past the flat muscles in his stomach, and I see his length, extended toward me as his hands rub along my thighs.

He moves off the bed and I watch his body, caught in flashes of the storm, as he retrieves something from his bag on the floor. When he returns, he holds a bottle of liquid in his hands and drops some condoms on the bedside table.

As he stands at the side of the bed, I try to keep my eyes on the ceiling. He opens the bottle and pours some liquid into his hand, before bending down to kiss my chin.

"Good girl," he says, "Watch."

His fingers move into the opening between my legs again, this time cold and slippery with the oily liquid. He massages my sex, as he bends over me and takes my nipple in his mouth. With his hand inside me, and his hot mouth against me, another moan escapes my throat. I press my hips into his hand.

"Do you want me to stop?" he asks, pausing his fingers.

"No," I pant. There is nothing left in my vocabulary but the feeling of his fingers, his tongue, his lips.

"I'll go slow," he says, as he climbs over my legs and spreads me apart. He kneels again, between my knees, rolling on a condom before stroking his covered length with more of the liquid. He bends down to kiss me, and I feel him tap against the opening of my sex, like a hard, slippery pole.

"Open your eyes," he says. His face is right over mine, his hand down between our legs, guiding himself against me. "If it's too fast, say so."

I clamp my eyes shut, and he doesn't ask me to open them again. Instead, he kisses me, nipping my lip as his tip enters me. I run my hands up his arms, to his shoulders, digging my fingernails into him as he pushes a little deeper inside me. My fingernails don't stop him, and I panic.

"I can't," I howl. "I can't!"

"Shhh," he soothes me. He doesn't withdraw, but he doesn't go any further. He strokes my hair, kisses the corners of my eyes, and he breathes out a whisper, "Relax."

"I can't!" I yelp, as he shifts and presses in a little deeper. I dig my fingernails into the thick muscles across his back, and feel him flinch, but he doesn't stop.

"Relax, Hale," he says. "It will hurt if you don't."

"It already hurts," I say.

"I won't go any deeper, until you're ready," he promises, and he ducks his head down toward my chest. His hair tickles against my chin, as his mouth settles over my right breast. All I can concentrate on his the baseball bat between my legs, until his tongue swivels over my nipple. He sucks the tiny button, teasing it up to a sharp point. I pull down on his shoulders, to draw his mouth closer. He moves his head to my other breast and repeats the agonizingly delicious sequence. When he finally lifts his mouth from me, I arch my back for more. Oscar captures my mouth, and bites down on the edge of my lower lip, as he thrusts deep inside me.

I suck in a breath, and rake my nails down his back. He grunts with the pain, but he begins a slow, lazy rhythm, grinding in and out of me. It hurts, but at the same time, it almost feels good. He stares down at me, and I'm worried I'm doing it wrong. I still don't squirm beneath him, because I'm sure it will hurt.

"It's never felt this good before," he whispers.

I draw his mouth down to meet mine. Catching his bottom lip, I suck it into my mouth gently, tugging it, and rubbing it with my tongue. Oscar groans. He drops onto his elbows with his release. When he opens his eyes, he's smiling. He takes my head in his hands and kisses me.

"Are you okay?" he asks. "Did you like it?"

I'm too sore to move my legs, but I still tell him the truth. "Yes," I say.

CHAPTER SIXTEEN

I WAKE UP BESIDE HIM, feeling weird. He is lying on his back, his face tipped away from me, asleep. The top sheet is draped just over his waist, but I can tell he's still naked.

I want to sneak away, to see how I've changed. I'm worried that the sheets will look like we spilled a bucket of red paint, but when I slide out and peek at them, there is only a tiny drop of red in the whole, ocean of white. I straighten up, realizing two things. One, is that I can't find my nightgown and, two, everything from the waist down is a little stiff and sore. It doesn't matter. Oscar's still asleep. I turn and hobble, naked, toward the stairs.

"You're so damn beautiful," Oscar says, behind me. I look over one shoulder, feeling the deep red blush sink into every cheek I have. He's still lying in bed, but he's turned on his side, toward me, and he's smiling. He repeats each word, drawing them out. "So. Damn. Beautiful."

"I was just..."

"Go," he says. "I just want to watch you walk away."

I escape down the stairs, with a smile on my own face, but when I hit the bathroom, I'm disappointed. There is nothing in my reflection that shows how different I feel this morning. It's like staring at a stranger in the mirror, because who I used to be, shouldn't be there anymore. My regular, old face should be replaced with a woman who knows what it is like to have sex.

I climb the stairs back to the bedroom. I want to strut into the room, confident and womanly, but I don't think I could pull it off. Instead, I peek around the corner first, to see if Oscar is watching. He's not. His head is on his pillow, nose toward the ceiling, eyes closed.

I scurry toward the edge of the bed, hoping to make it before he opens his eyes and turns his head to me. I don't. He pops his eyes open and I nearly shriek. A smile spreads over his face, and his eyes sweep over my naked body.

"You okay?"

"Mmm hmm," I say, diving between the sheets. He turns toward his bedside table, to check the time on his phone, and that's when I see the long, raking cuts in his back. The sheet beneath him is speckled with his blood, not mine. I groan. "I wrecked your back."

"I know," he says, laying back and reaching for me. He doesn't seem upset at all. Then he smirks, "It's only fair. I wrecked your virginity."

I half-laugh, pushing his face away. When I lay back on the pillow, there is a lump. Reaching underneath, I extract my nightgown.

"Oh, good," I say, but Oscar grabs the bunch of fabric and throws it off the end of the bed.

"No clothes," he says. "I don't allow clothes in my bed."

I pull the sheet up over me, but he pulls me closer. He presses my hips against his, and he groans.

"No more," I say. He groans again.

"Fine. Not now," he says. "But soon."

A delicious drop of adrenaline races through me, and I think: maybe the woman I couldn't see in the mirror is in here after all. I snuggle closer, replaying last night in my head, as I inadvertently rub up against him.

"Last warning," he mumbles.

"Alright, alright," I say, and lie still.

"I was thinking we could go home today," he sighs into my hair and I feel an unexpected twinge of sadness over the idea. I wouldn't admit it out loud, but last night was exciting, and I want it to happen again. There won't be any hope of that, if I have to pack up, drive back, and get dropped off at my father's house. It will be an agonizing wait, to be with Oscar again, until we are married. The idea of packing exhausts me. I never want to leave this bed.

"I don't want to go," I say.

"No?" he says. "You're having second thoughts about marrying me?"

"No," I say, surprised that he'd think that. Especially now. Especially with my naked rear pressed into his lap. "I just don't want to go home. I...I don't want to be away from you."

"That's what you thought? You're not going home, Hale. You've got a new home now. With me. We'll be staying at my father's house, until we find our own place. We've got to start house hunting right after we're married. It's going to be busy when we get back."

"Let's just stay here," I say, and his laugh is so deep that I feel it roll through my back and into my stomach.

"It would be nice," he says. "But it will be even better, once you have my last name, and we're in our own house, and our own bed. We've got a lot to get done first, though. Where do you want to go for our honeymoon?"

I blush, but I'm not looking at him, so I whisper, "To bed."

Oscar pulls me even closer, his hand moving like fire over my skin.

\#

The second time feels better than the first, but when I get out of bed, I move so slowly across the floor that it worries Oscar. I take a shower, and by the time I come out, he's packed up our things, emptied a lot of the fridge into garbage bags, and has everything ready to go. He has a box of donuts on the table for me, along with his phone, and a glass of milk.

"Just relax and talk to Sher while I grab a shower, okay?" he says. I take a seat at the table, as he goes into the bathroom and turns on the water. The phone rings, as I finish my donut. The screen says DAD, and I think of just letting it go to voicemail, but it's Oscar's dad, so it could be important. I pick up.

"Hello?" I say, and the voice that greets me is accusatory.

"Who is this?"

"Hale," I say.

"Oh," Mr. Maree says. His voice drops to a pleasant tone. "Hello, Hale. How are you?"

"Fine," I say.

"Where's Oscar?"

"Oh, um," I stammer. How can I say his son's in the shower? My entire face burns what is probably a fuschia color. Mr. Maree probably hears it in my voice. My new, woman voice. I stumble for what to say and come up with nothing but the truth. I frown as I tell Oscar's dad, "He's in the shower."

"Oh." It's Mr. Maree's turn to stammer. "Well, could you have his call me when he's—through?"

"I will," I say, wincing hard once the words are out.

"Alright then. It was nice talking with you, Hale."

"You too. Bye!" I wince again and hang up. I drop Oscar's phone on the table and a sqwerky shiver rolls through me. It's not like Mr. Maree wouldn't expect any of this. He practically insisted on it. But knowing that we all share a secret that we are never going to discuss openly is weird too.

Oscar emerges from the bathroom, his black hair still wet, although he's fully dressed. And now, when I look at him, I see so much more than just the way his shirt hugs his arms and chest, or the way his shorts fit him. Now I know just how powerful and gorgeous his body is, under all those clothes. And I flush, thinking about what a crime it is to ever cover that body up.

"Ready to go?" he says.

"Sure. Your father called."

"You talked to him?"

"Yeah. He just said to have you call him."

"Then I'll do that," he says, landing a kiss on my sugared lips. "Mmm. Cinnamon sugar."

He slips his phone from his pocket, and calls his father.

"Hey, Dad," he says, pacing closer to the windows facing the beach. I trace the width of his shoulders, appreciating how his back plunges into his narrow waist. I remember how I laid on the bed, watching his incredible backside in the mirror overhead, as he pushed himself into me.

"We're coming back today," he says, turning, and I snap out of my daydream. He grins at me as he continues talking to his father. "Yes, that would be fine. I think we're only looking for an intimate gathering though. Well, that's not intimate. I don't know, I could ask her."

Oscar presses *mute* and says, "My father wants to throw us a reception, Hale. What do you think?"

"I don't have many people to invite," I shrug. "My dad, Sher's family, that's about it."

"That's fine. My father would like us to have the wedding ceremony on our grounds, followed by an outdoor reception. What do you think?"

I shrug. I have no idea. I've never been to a wedding, not even my mother's. "Good, I guess."

"She said that's fine, Dad," Oscar says into the phone. He laughs. "Don't get too outrageous, okay?...No, Dad...that's outrageous...that too...we'll talk when we get back, alright?"

#

I sleep too long. I miss the ride home, and feel bad when I wake up just as Oscar's arms slide around me from the open, truck door. We're only feet from the Maree's front entrance.

"What are you doing?"

"I didn't think you were going to wake up."

"I'm awake," I say, sliding out onto the driveway beside him, but when I wobble on the ground, Oscar takes me up into his arms anyway.

"I should carry you over the threshold," he grins. I am surprised at how easy it is to relax in his arms, breathing in the deep scent of the cologne I gave him.

The door opens just as we reach it, and I recognize Mr. Maree from the night in my kitchen. He is in a suit, his body held stiffly, the whites of his eyes are white instead of bloodshot. He steps aside, so Oscar can carry me in and set me down in the enormous entryway. Oscar stays close, his arm around my waist.

"Good trip?" Mr. Maree asks, and Oscar nods.

"I slept all the way back," I say. I don't know why I needed to say that. Mr. Maree takes it in stride.

"Well, I suppose that's the life of a newlywed," he says kindly. "How about you show Hale to the guest house, Oscar, and we'll have a talk before dinner. Hale, I hope you enjoy mesquite chicken. I am looking forward to discussing the wedding party then."

With that, Mr. Maree turns and walks away, and Oscar says, "We're staying in the guest house until we find our own place. It's more private that way."

He leads me through his mansion to the back patio. We walk through French doors, and down a cobbled garden path to another house. What they call a 'guest house' looks like a regular house to me, even if the mansion dwarfs it. It's charming, with a front porch that stretches around the entire exterior, and enough trees to seclude it from the mansion.

Oscar opens the front door and lifts me over the threshold again. He sets me down inside, on a polished, wood floor that has a better shine than my own hair. To the right, there are two steps leading down to the white carpet of the living room, straight forward is a kitchen, and to the left are three doors, one that leads into an enormous bedroom, one that opens to a bathroom, and the other that leads into a den.

With his fingertips, Oscar takes me into the bedroom. The bed has a metal canopy draped around the top with white lace. There is a walk-in closet, and a door leading into the bathroom.

"If you want to relax in the tub, I'll bring in our bags," Oscar says. He opens the door to a raised tub that is large enough for five people.

"It's a swimming pool," I say. Oscar laughs and turns on the water, tossing in some of the bath beads from a dish on the ledge. I guess I'm taking a bath.

"I'll join you in a minute," he whispers, leaving a kiss on my neck, and then he is gone, back out the door to get the bags.

#

There are no bubbles. None. And there is a huge stained glass window that lets so much light in, it's like being outside. Without bubbles to hide beneath. The bath beads only scent the water, so by the time the tub fills up, Oscar is back, and I'm still standing there, chewing on my thumbnail.

"What's the matter?" he asks.

"Oh, um, I thought there'd be bubbles," I say.

"Those aren't, huh?" He points to the dish of bath beads and I shake my head. "Huh, well, they smell good."

He strips off his shirt easily, but pauses when he sees that I'm still standing there, gnawing my thumb. He reaches up and moves my hand away from my mouth.

"You okay?" he asks.

"It's really bright in here," I tell him.

"Good." He smiles shamelessly. "Why did you think I wanted to take a bath in here?"

He steps toward me, reaching for the waistband of my shorts. I let him undress me and do the same to him, although I don't look. I keep my gaze rooted in his, and he does the same. But being naked in front of Oscar, with his eyes never once wandering from mine, is even more intense than if he were kneeling between my legs, watching his own finger moving in and out of me.

We step up into the bath together, and lower into the warm water at once. Oscar takes my hands and drapes them over his shoulders. He sits on the ledge beneath the waterline, and pulls me on top of him, so my knees are on either side of his hips. Without ever taking his eyes off mine, he lowers me down onto his lap.

I feel his manhood pressing up toward me. He lowers me down on the tip slowly, but it hurts as he enters me. I bite my lip.

"That hurts?" he asks. I shake my head, but as he moves more deeply inside me, I have to bite harder to stop myself from whimpering.

"No, no," Oscar says, pulling out of me. "If it hurts, we've got to stop and let you heal."

He draws me close and kisses me. "We're not doing this because I want it. We do this because *we* want it. Understand?"

I nod, and he kisses me again.

#

Stepping into the dining room in the Maree mansion, I feel totally underdressed. The table is made of dark, polished wood, and it's set with fine china. Mr. Maree is still wearing his suit, his polished shoes, and every strand of his hair is in place. The only thing that keeps me from running away is Oscar, standing beside me in shorts too.

Oscar pulls out a chair for me, and takes the one beside it for himself. Mr. Maree takes a seat too, just as a woman in cotton capris and a blue t-shirt comes in with a tray of salads. She serves us the salads, along with a basket of bread, and fills our water glasses.

"Your dinner will be ready in a moment," she says. "Anyone need anything else before then? Mr. Maree? Oscar? Hale?"

"No thank you, Linda," Mr. Maree and Oscar answer, almost at once. I'm shocked that she knows my name, but I just shake my head with a shy smile. She smiles too, and excuses herself from the room with her empty tray.

"So, we're having a wedding," Mr. Maree says. "Has Oscar told you my suggestion? I was thinking we could have the ceremony on the grounds and have an outdoor reception."

"That sounds sweet," I say.

"Excellent," Mr. Maree says. "Then we'll send you for a dress tomorrow, and I'll let Holly know to go ahead with the arrangements for a Sunday wedding."

If I had food in mouth, I'd choke. That means we have one day to get ready. The only comfort I have is from the conversations I've overheard between Oscar and his father. The wedding will be a small gathering in the back yard, nothing much, so maybe it will only take a day to prepare. I can't imagine many guests coming, on a day's notice. I'm sure my father will be there, but I'm not sure how I feel about that just yet. Our last conversation ended with him rifling a bottle at the wall beside me.

"Sunday is perfect," I say, and Mr. Maree grins.

"Generally speaking, weddings are reserved for Saturdays, however, this is a particularly special occasion," he says. I think he's going to mention Rick Tatum, and how we need to hurry everything along to seal our families together, or more like, seal my and my father's mouths shut, but Mr. Maree turns his eyes lovingly to his son, and I realize instantly that I assumed wrong. "It's not everyday that my only son gets married, and you'll see Hale, that being a Maree means that sometimes, not very often, but sometimes, we can tell the world that Sunday is actually Saturday, and they will agree."

I am in awe of what that means. I can't even tell the guy at the bakery that his three-day-old bread should be marked down.

"Let's see," Mr. Maree says, retrieving his phone. He mumbles as he scrolls his phone screen, "Holly sent me questions to move things along. Ah yes. Colors. What color preference do you have, Hale?"

"Purple," Oscar answers, at the same time that I say, "Yellow."

"Hmm," Mr. Maree says, texting. "Purple and yellow. Any preferences for music or table arrangements?"

I have no idea what I would prefer. A stereo? Flowers? I don't know a thing about flowers. The only two I can identify are roses and dandelions.

"Whatever you think is best," I say, and Mr. Maree smiles at me.

"Any preference for the main dishes?"

"I don't know," I say, glancing at Oscar, but he just shrugs, encouraging me to answer. "I haven't been to any weddings. I know they had mostaccioli at a baby shower I went to."

"You're certainly easy to get along with, Hale," Mr. Maree says. "I can tell that it will be a pleasure to have you in our family."

"Thank you," I say. I don't know what to call him. Sir? Mr. Maree? Dad? I just steer around it by taking a drink of water. I glance over at Oscar and see him watching me with a tiny grin. I mouth to him, *what?* as his father texts something into his phone.

Beautiful, Oscar mouths back, with a wink that heats me up inside.

"Oh," Mr. Maree looks up from his phone. "Your friend, Sher, has chosen some dress ideas, it seems. Holly has also informed the dress shop that you're coming."

"I'll take her there tomorrow," Oscar says.

"Alright," Mr. Maree says, glancing at his son with a smile. "And what about you, Oscar? Holly's got ideas for your tuxedo style, but I told her you would want some say in the matter. I assume I'm right?"

"You are," Oscar says. "I'll talk with Holly myself."

"Perfect," Mr. Maree says. He clicks in another text and lays the phone down beside his plate. "People say weddings are nightmares to plan. I just don't see it."

"That's because it's Holly's nightmare, not yours," Oscar laughs. His father replies with a chuckle, sliding a bite of salad into his mouth.

"One last bit of business, Hale," Mr. Maree says, after Linda delivers our main course. "I've spoken to your father, and I understand that the two of you left on, well, not the best of terms."

I push the green beans across my plate with my fork. My father gave me to a stranger. No, he *threw me out* to be with a stranger. I might have fallen in love with the stranger and agreed to be his wife, but what if I hadn't? Should that even matter now?

"He'd like to have a word with you," Mr. Maree says. "Actually, I think it is more accurate to say he'd like to apologize to you. He's doing well, and I hope you won't mind that I invited him here tonight for dessert."

"Um," I glance at Mr. Maree, and at Oscar, and back again. "I guess that's fine."

And then, for the rest of dinner, I hear only bits of the conversation, as my mind turns over what exactly I'm going to say to my father.

CHAPTER SEVENTEEN

MY FATHER COMES IN AT the same time that Linda brings in dessert, as if he'd been waiting somewhere else. I think it is just a dessert tray full of choices, but Mr. Maree explains that they are cake samples. He thinks it would be a 'nice experience' for all of us to try the different bakery samples, and choose which one we want, as a family, for the wedding.

My dad sidles up to the table, twisting his baseball cap in his hands. He looks different. Taller, somehow. He's gained some weight, and his skin doesn't look so ruddy. But it's not until he bends down and pecks my cheek that I know what the real difference is.

He's sober.

"Hello, Hale," he says, taking the empty seat beside me. "How are you?"

"Getting married, Dad. How are you?"

"Getting sober, honey." He looks into his lap, and I worry he might be about to cry. If he cries, I'm going to cry, and it will be a mess. I'm relieved when he lifts his head and pulls it together. "Are you happy?"

I sit for a minute, unsure of what to say, whether I need to pursue the fight or let it go. But Oscar's thigh brushes mine, and when I glance at him, he gives me an encouraging wink that decides it all.

"I'm very happy, Dad, thank you," I say, and my father looks away and pinches his eyes.

"Good," he says, but his voice crumbles. "Hale, I'm..."

"Dad," I lay a hand on his arm. "It's fine. I'm happy."

My father gives me a bittersweet grin, and Mr. Maree takes over then, with an elegant smile. He taps his fork on the edge of one of the plates.

"This one," he says, "is incredible. This is the hazelnut cake, with a praline and chocolate buttercream, I think."

Oscar passes me the plate. I put a piece of the cake in my mouth, and it is exactly what Mr. Maree said—incredible. I close my eyes for a moment to savor it. I've never tasted a dessert as good as this.

"Try it, Dad," I say, handing him the plate. "This is the one I'd like at my wedding. I think you'll like it too."

My father takes a bite, his lips trembling as he closes his mouth on the sweet sample.

"I do," he says, with a grateful smile. "Thank you, Hale. I like it very much."

#

The next morning, Sher is waiting at the doors of the dress shop, where Oscar drops me off. She squeals when she sees me, and runs to throw her arms around me.

"I missed you! I missed you!" she shrieks. "And I'm so excited! A Sunday wedding? It's so elegant! Do you know you made the news?"

"Get out of here!" I say.

Sher puts on an announcer's voice, and says, into the imaginary microphone of her curled fist, *"Otto Maree, of Otto Maree Investments, announced today that his only son, Oscar Charles Maree, will be wedding a Miss Hale Simmons, in a Sunday ceremony, to be held on the grounds of the family's estate. The entire Maree Investment firm, and their subsidiary companies, are not expected to report back to work until Wednesday, in order to celebrate, as they say, 'properly'."* Sher drops her fist microphone. "That is so over the top! You are so lucky, Hale!"

And I haven't even told her how I left her behind in Virginville yet. The idea of telling her all about Sophia and Amy streaks across my mind, but I can't think of a way to tell her without having to tell everything, so I just keep my mouth shut. Instead, I just smile, and we both stand back to look around the shop.

"Can you believe this place?" I gape.

Sher does the same, finishing my thought, "It's so fancy!"

A sales woman scoops us up almost immediately. Her sparkling, silver-bar name pin is embossed with the name, 'Milan', in black print. She looks to be only a little older than us, but just by her perfectly fitted clothes, flawless make-up, and incredible shoes, Sher and I both agree immediately, in glances to one another, that we want to grow up to be Milan someday. She even pronounces her name stylishly, *Mee-lon*.

She asks me about dress styles, and colors, and when all she gets from me is a blank stare, Sher steps in and saves me. She fishes a folded pile of magazine pages from her purse, and some of the smaller clippings fall out and flutter to the floor. Milan helps us pick them up, and takes the mess of scraps to the counter. She lays them out, and we all look them over. In minutes, Milan is talking to us as if we all grew up together.

"Oh, I love this," I say, pointing to one of the three bridesmaids dresses that Sher clipped.

"That's my favorite too!" Sher says, and Milan smiles as she picks up the picture.

"I think I have the perfect dress," she says. "And what about you, Hale? What kind of dresses do you like? I understand the wedding is tomorrow, so I suppose we should look at what we have in your size. I know Mr. Maree said that he would pay for speed alterations, but it's not always that easy. Luckily, with your particular size, we've got a great selection available."

Milan takes us to a room with dresses that line the wall. The first one I see is a fitted, sleeveless dress that spreads out more fully at the bottom. Sher pulls in a dramatic breath, as I pull the dress from the row.

"That's gorgeous!" she says. Milan starts explaining what kind of dress it is: a mermaid dress, with a heart-shaped bodice. She says things like brocade, and crystals, and tulle, but all I want to know is if the dress will fit, and if I can afford to buy it.

Once it's on, I spin in a mirror, and Sher says, "That's the one," over and over again, until I say, "You're right."

"You couldn't have chosen a better dress to suit your figure," Milan says. "This style is both elegant and sexy. I hope that is what you were going for."

Milan takes the dress when I'm done.

"It will be cleaned and delivered to your house in the morning, as will Sher's dress," she says.

"How much do we owe?" I ask, and Milan brushes away the air with her fingers.

"Nothing," she says. "Mr. Maree is taking care of the bill."

Sher squeals and hops and tells me again, how lucky I am. Its finally starting to sink in, just how lucky that is.

#

Oscar and I don't eat dinner with Mr. Maree. Instead, we eat sandwiches on the back porch of the guest house. The backyard is so secluded by trees and shrubs, that it feels like we're the only two people left in this beautiful little patch of the world.

"Are you overwhelmed yet?" he asks, bumping me with his knee. I look into his eyes, and it's like they swallow me up. I don't have any interest in looking away.

"Not at all," I say. "Are you?"

"No," he chuckles, "all I have to do is meet you at the altar, right?"

"That's pretty much all I have to do too," I say.

"Does that bother you?"

"No. Why would it?"

"Well, I know girls usually want a lot of say about their wedding day. It's kind of a big deal, isn't it? They make TV shows about what a big deal it is."

I shrug. "It's just one day," I say. "The big deal is all the days after."

Oscar reaches out, his fingertips curling under my chin, and he kisses me.

"I love you." He says it so simply, it's like he says it every day. "You're not a bridezilla."

But it's the 'I love you' part that catches me. He doesn't say it every day. He's never even said it before. And he just looks away, like it's no big deal that it's the first time he's said that, and like it's not an even bigger deal that I'm not jumping to say it back. All he does is look out into the trees, and takes a bite of his sandwich.

I climb into his lap, wrapping my legs around his back.

"Hi there," he says with a grin, once I'm sitting face to face with him.

"Oscar," I say. "You just said something really serious."

"Hmm," he says, nodding and licking the mustard from his lip. "I did, didn't I?"

"You did," I say.

His eyes graze over how our bodies are smashed together. "It looks like you have something you want to say about it?"

"Yes," I say, looking over his shoulder. "I don't want to say 'I love you' for any of the wrong reasons."

"Well," he says, "I think any reason I give you is a pretty good one."

"Not if it's based on your looks, or your money, or because some guy died at a bar, where our dads were having a drink."

He thinks for a moment, and then his eyes are on mine, the intensity a little startling. "Is that *all* the reasons I've given you?"

"No, but," I squirm, uneasy with the words, but Oscar holds me to him.

"Go on," he says, even though his tone is curious, instead of angry.

"I just don't want to start throwing those words around. It means something, you know?"

"It means everything," he says softly, and then his hands are in my hair. "That's why I said it."

He pulls me into a kiss, but when our lips part, I breathe, "I love you."

"No, no," he murmurs. "Not for this. Say it when you mean *all of it*. I already know you love me for this."

And he lies back on the hard wood porch, pulling me down with him, in the very last light of evening that filters through the trees.

#

I wake to the sound of machinery. Not coffee pots or washing machines, but real machinery, the massive kind that earns the name. Oscar is not beside me in bed, so I get up, pull on my clothes, and look out the window. It sounds like there is a forklift coming at the house, but there is nothing to see out the bedroom window. I cross the foyer and go into the living room, which is lined with windows, and immediately see what woke me.

A guy on a Hi-Lo is moving stacks of tables onto the main lawn. I rub my eyes. The Hi-Lo is still there, carefully shoveling the pile of tables off the machine's front prongs.

"Oscar?" I call, and turn as he emerges from the kitchen with a mug of coffee.

"Right here," he says. He crosses the carpet to stand beside me, sipping his coffee and watching the workers that are flooding the lawn with chairs and flowers, as an enormous tent rises up off the lawn to the far left.

"What is all this?" I ask.

"Our wedding," he says.

"All of this? It's a Sunday wedding! This looks like a circus is coming!"

Oscar chuckles. "A circus *is* coming," he says. "There are about five hundred guests invited."

"Six..." I cough. "Six *hundred?* Who? How do you even know five hundred people?"

"Success with Fortune 500 companies, Hale. They get you known."

"Oh my God," I say, smashing a hand to my forehead. "I thought it was going to be like ten people, twenty tops. Not five hundred. Oh my God."

"Come on and sit down," Oscar says, putting his coffee on a table. "That's just the reception. There are only about a hundred invited to the actual wedding."

"Only?" I say. Oscar takes my hands in his and kisses my knuckles. The warmth of his mouth centers me again, and I can breathe.

"Don't think of it," he says. "It's just going to be a wonderful party, that's all. You get to wear a beautiful dress, and Sher and your father will be here. We'll dance and eat great food, and people will be tripping over themselves to meet you. You won't remember any of their names, and when it's all over, we'll just be Mr. and Mrs. Maree. House hunters. Honeymooners. Arguers of how-many-children-we're-not-having-yet. Just that, Hale. Nothing more."

"It seems like everything." I say.

"Well, it is everything," he says, kissing my knuckles again. "But it's nothing to be afraid of."

"And you'll be there," I say, with a weak smile.

"Of course. I'll always be there," he says.

CHAPTER EIGHTEEN

I WISH I COULD REMEMBER everything, but it goes by in a blur. Sher and I spend most of the day at a spa. It sounds lovely, except that the closer we get to the actual wedding time, at five in the evening, the more nervous I get. I can't enjoy the massage, or the pedicure, or the manicure, or the hairstyling, or the incredibly appealing way a man named Marco does my make-up. I don't look like myself, or feel like myself, and by the time that I'm standing in my dress, at the mansion French doors that lead to the rose-scattered runner, I'm beyond terrified. I'm not sure I'll make it to Oscar, who is waiting at the other end.

It's not that I don't want to marry him.

It's not that I won't keep the secret.

It's not that I'm angry with my father, or worried that I won't be able to be everything I wanted to.

It's none of that.

It's just that my legs feel like string, and my body feels like lead, and that makes it tough to get where I need to go.

My father takes my arm as the music starts, and Sher squeals the last squeal I'll hear as a single woman, before she disappears out the French doors. My father smells faintly of booze. He apologizes. He promises he'll get his act together. He says he is proud of me.

We walk.

The runner dips under my shoes a little. A hundred faces turn from their decorated chairs on either side of the lawn, to smile at me. I am afraid of throwing up. I am scared of wiping out in front of these hundred smiling faces. I am terrified that someone will take a picture, if I do.

Oscar comes into view. He's beyond incredible, in his black tux with a silver and black embossed vest. He's got a dark purple flower in his lapel. Any girl would feel blessed to be on her way to marry him, and I'd like to say that the sight of him makes it all better, but he looks worried when he spots me too. I wobble once on my heels, and although my father manages to hold me steady, I see Oscar lurch forward a little, hands up, as if he would be able to reach me, and catch me, if I fell.

It's the first time in my life I wish I were drunk. My hands are sweating, as I hold my gorgeous bouquet of purple and yellow flowers. I don't even know what they're called. The wedding planner woman told me to keep the bouquet at my waist, but with every step forward, the flowers seem to get a little higher, as if I'll end up peeking out of them, once I reach Oscar.

"Dad," I whisper, "I don't think I'm going to make it."

"I don't think I can either, Hale, but we're going to have to. Almost there. Hang on, okay?"

I think he's being metaphorical. I don't know. All I can really concentrate on is not throwing up in my purple and yellow flowers.

We reach the end, and the Pastor asks who's giving me away, twice, without any answer from my father. My dad's just standing beside me, looking pale. The Pastor finally asks my dad directly, "Mr. Simmons, will you give your daughter to be wed?"

My father looks like he's going to lose it. I lean over and instead of kissing his cheek, I whisper hotly in his ear, "Say yes, Dad! You're not even the one who needs to be drunk—I am! Just hold it together so I don't come totally unglued, for God's sake!"

My father straightens up, clears his throat, and tells the Pastor, "I do", as he hands me over to Oscar. Oscar's strong hand on my arm snaps something into place. Not completely, but almost. His fingertips are soft, and his smile is genuine as he leans over and whispers in my ear, "You're gorgeous, Hale. We're going to get through this together, okay?"

"Okay," I say, a little too loudly. There are some titters from the decorated chairs. The Pastor begins, and I rock on my heels. Oscar keeps a hand on my elbow, although I don't think we're supposed to be touching yet. The Pastor looks over the top of his Bible, and asks the crowd if anyone objects to us being married, but his eyes fall back on me, as if he thinks I've got something to say.

I don't, but there is a disturbance behind us, and I hear the words, clear as bells, "I object."

Oscar and I turn together, my eyes running over the rows of heads, to find the one that is out of place. It's not hard to find her at all, standing like the blond Popsicle stick she is, in the middle of the crowd of guests.

"Amy," Oscar growls. She's dragged her scandal all the way here, and now she's going to make sure to wave it around in broad daylight.

"Go home, Amy, you're not welcome here," Oscar says.

"That's a shame, Oscar, because I think everyone would like to know about us." Her smile spreads, like marshmallows on a radiator.

"What the hell?" My father rises from his seat, swinging around to face her.

"There is no 'us'," Oscar growls again, ignoring the murmurs that pop up among the rows of guests.

"Young lady," Mr. Maree stands from his seat to face Amy too. I'm sure Oscar has told him who she is. That's probably why Mr. Maree looks so pale. "You are not welcome to stay, if you intend to ruin my son's wedding."

"I'm here because he killed a man, and tried to cover it up," Amy blurts.

"Where's security?" my father shouts. "This girl is nuts!"

"Rick Tatum!" Amy shrieks. "Oscar killed him!"

People's heads are whipping back and forth, trying to catch all the reactions.

"Who the hell is Rick Tatum?" Oscar says. "I don't even know the person you're talking about!"

Technically, Oscar's telling the truth, but the whispers still hike up and somebody says, "Isn't that the guy that was killed at Modo's Bar?"

I assume that the man who stands up next is Modo. He's a burly guy with long hair, tied back in a ponytail for the occasion. He's wearing a nice suit, and a scowl aimed at Amy, as he says, "The guy that died outside my bar died of natural causes. He had a seizure and clonked his head. The cops released the autopsy report this morning. So, what are you talking about, little girl?"

"He didn't hit his head! He came after Oscar! Oscar did it!" Amy shrieks, but it's obvious that she's losing ground. Her eyes dart around, and people point at her, whispering things about sanity.

"Young lady," Mr. Maree says over the murmuring, "are you accusing my son of someone's accidental death? I don't take kindly to that."

"He came after Oscar!" Amy shouts.

Someone in the crowd calls out, "How do you know that, Amy?" The voice is familiar. I scan through the unfamiliar faces and find the slightly familiar one. Sophia.

She's standing in the back, in a pristine, pink dress. And she repeats, like a brick wall, "How do you know that he was after Oscar, Amy?"

Amy spots Sophia, and begins sliding past people, toward the end of the aisle.

"How do you know, unless you sent the guy, Amy?" Sophia calls. The whispers jump up, and I catch bits and pieces of insinuations and accusations pointed in Amy's direction, instead of at Oscar, or his father. The words *set up* drift through the crowd, and the acknowledgement bubbles up over and over again, that the Marees are good men, solid men, not men that would do this sort of thing. The final conclusion seems to be that this poor young woman must be a jilted lover, who has come to air her grievance over not being in the bride's dress.

Amy is shamed, and practically discounted, before she even scoots out to the end of the aisle. She walks quickly back toward the French doors of the main house, but Mr. Maree raises his hand to one of the Security guards, and the guard murmurs into his headpiece. Two more guards materialize, on either side of Amy, and escort her out. Sophia takes a seat, demurely, in the back, blowing a kiss off her hand to Oscar, and then another, with a friendly wink, to me.

The Pastor leans down and says, "Are you ready to resume?"

But Oscar lifts two fingers to the Pastor, and the Holy Man nods and steps back, giving us as much privacy as can be had, while standing in front of a hundred expectant faces. Oscar bends, so his lips are near my ear.

"You don't have to marry me." he says. His voice cracks. "Tatum died of a seizure, not the impact of the fall. I found out this morning. There's nothing to hide now. My father would deny the accident, but there is no evidence against him anyway. I should have told you, but I didn't, because I was afraid I'd lose you, Hale. But this isn't fair to you either. I'll see to it that your father is helped, and that you have enough to go to a good college. You're free to go. I won't hold you to a marriage you don't want."

"You won't?" I say.

"No." His voice cracks again, as he shakes his head and looks away. I look out over the hundred guests, and then I glance over my shoulder at Sher, who smiles a sad smile, like she'll love me no matter what I do. I turn back to Oscar, but his eyes are cast down.

I lean closer to him and whisper, "But what if I said I want to marry you? What if I said I want to marry you because I love the man that you are? What if I said I love you, Oscar?"

He finally looks back up, meeting my gaze.

"Then I'd come running," he says.

"Then let me," I say. "Because I love you, Oscar. I want to marry you, and be your wife, and argue about children. I want everything about you. I do."

I drop my purple-and-yellow bouquet, and forget all about what we're supposed to do and say next. Instead, in front of God and our hundred witnesses, I reach for my husband, and he encircles me in his arms, kissing me, in a way that means absolutely everything.

SPECIAL THANKS

Thank you, God.

Love and thanks to Pook, who takes on the world for me, with me. You're always my hero.

Thanks to Mom, who insisted on helping to edit HALE. I love you dearly although we can never look each other in the eyes again.

Thanks to Ma and Pa and Dad, for the unwavering belief and the unspoken agreement at family get-togethers that none of us have ever written or read this book.

Huge thanks to PepsiCoke (J Nunez); 4AM (M Anderson); Candace; Novels on the Run's Michelle; my Debbie Ulbrich; Michelle Leighton; Annie (all rosies) (AM Hargrove); SupaGurl Heather; Flyleaf's Heather R.; M. Smith (my fave Book Nerd in America); Love of Book's Christy; Supernatural Snark's Jenny; Tess; Globug & HootieGirl; H. Rosdol; my absolute fave Tsk Tsk girls Kathryn & Shelley (I'll bring David back soonish! Maybe!); Kat Ellis; Shelly Crane; Mark "McThrashbone" Morgan; Fighting Dreamer Cayce; Rainy Day Heidi; Captivated Reading Christy; Jen Kromer; Turning Pages Angela; EJ Wesley; Reading Angel Angela; Book Addict Tee; Clare Davidson; Lita; Howie; Kristina; Autumn; Rebecca E; M Fita; KSauce; J Betcher; Sue & Chris Salah; Dani; Pam Heintz; L Zera; Starla Huchton who has a voice like absolute buttah; Soda & Brend...and to all those I missed, but am eternally grateful~ you know who you are.

And thank you to you, with your eyes on these pages, for reading. I hope this story brings you joy.

Made in the USA
Lexington, KY
06 November 2012